"You seem very keen to go home on weekends."

Kirby stiffened. Had he found out about Meg? She would not tolerate snide comments about her daughter.

"I am keen," she acknowledged flatly.

"Is there a man, Kirby?"

Suddenly she understood. She could put what he had misunderstood to good use.

"Yes, there's a man." She lied without a qualm.

She was in danger. She did not want to feel. Feelings made one vulnerable, and she never wanted to feel vulnerable. Yet just the closeness of Ross's body was enough to make her feel. And if he knew how strongly he affected her, he would press his advantage and make love to her. Ross was a man wasn't he? And men took their fun where they could get it.

"Someone important?" he asked.

ROSEMARY CARTER started off writing short stories and for a long time received only rejections. The turnabout came at the end of her first pregnancy. "It is a memory I cherish," she says, "for the baby was born the day after the acceptance." She lives a few hours away from the Canadian Rockies, and she and her husband—tall and lean as her heroes—love exploring the beautiful mountain trails. But enchantment with her previous home has never waned and that is why she sets most of her books in the South African bushveld.

Books by Rosemary Carter

HARLEQUIN PRESENTS
615—LION'S DOMAIN
664—SERPENT IN PARADISE
752—LETTER FROM BRONZE MOUNTAIN
831—IMPETUOUS MARRIAGE
855—A FOREVER AFFAIR
880—PILLOW PORTRAITS

HARLEQUIN ROMANCE
1986—MAN OF THE WILD
2312—RETURN TO DEVIL'S VIEW
2380—MAN IN THE SHADOWS

These books may be available at your local bookseller.

Don't miss any of our special offers. Write to us at the following address for information on our newest releases.

Harlequin Reader Service
901 Fuhrmann Blvd., P.O. Box 1397, Buffalo, NY 14240
Canadian address: P.O. Box 2800, Postal Station A,
5170 Yonge St., Willowdale, Ont. M2N 6J3

ROSEMARY CARTER

pillow portraits

Harlequin Books

TORONTO • NEW YORK • LONDON
AMSTERDAM • PARIS • SYDNEY • HAMBURG
STOCKHOLM • ATHENS • TOKYO • MILAN

Harlequin Presents first edition May 1986
ISBN 0-373-10880-X

Original hardcover edition published in 1985
by Mills & Boon Limited

CHAPTER ONE

'THE boss wants to see you, Kirby.'

The slender girl with the wide green eyes and honey-coloured hair turned from her locker in surprise. 'Mr Anderson? What would he want of me at this time of the morning? Something wrong, do you think?'

Helen smiled as she looked up from the galleys she was proof-reading. 'He didn't seem more than usually abrupt, if that's what's bothering you. Perhaps he's about to offer you a raise.'

'Unlikely to say the least.'

Kirby tried to smile, but as she put down her bag she acknowledged to herself that she was worried. Landing the job at Anderson's Publishing had been a major turning-point in her life. It meant so much to her, she did not think she could bear it if something were to go wrong.

In the year that she'd been here it had grown to be more than a job, a nine-to-five routine to be forgotten when she went home at night. She was becoming passionately interested in the world of publishing. It was her dream to go from proof-reading to journalism. In her free time, when little Meg was asleep and the household chores were done, she wrote. Just last month her article on a female jockey had won an in-house award, and several of her interviews had appeared in the local papers.

It was one of those days when a strong wind blew through the streets of Cape Town, so Kirby stopped to check her appearance on the way to Mr Anderson's office. She did not think the image she saw in the mirror revealed her insecurities. Only she knew the economies she had practised to afford the well-cut cream suit and the silk blouse that matched her eyes. Tiny pearls studded ears left bare by hair that was swept upwards in a smooth chignon with just a few tendrils escaping to frame her face, and her make-up was discreet. She looked the way she wanted to look—like an efficient young career woman.

She hadn't always dressed so severely. There was a time when most of her clothes had been casual and her hair had hung loose to her shoulders. Then it hadn't mattered if men were attracted by her appearance. If they thought of her as a sex-object. One man in particular.

It mattered very much now.

Not that she even thought of herself as pretty any longer. But she was. Kirby did not realise how many men looked at her a second time after the first. They were men who saw behind the cool façade to the sadness that lurked sometimes in the lovely green eyes. There was a difference though. The men who looked at Kirby now were not the men who had looked at her three years ago. And that was something else Kirby did not know. She gave no man enough of her time to find out.

Her boss was such a man. Kirby's loveliness was never more pronounced than now, he thought, when the vulnerability she tried so hard to conceal from the world and herself was in evidence.

'I'm sorry I was late,' she said a little breathlessly, getting in the apology before he could speak. 'The traffic was bad.'

'A traffic-jam all the way up Adderley Street I believe,' he agreed mildly.

So she was not in trouble. Less warily, but no less expectantly, she waited for him to speak.

Hugh Anderson liked to come straight to the point. 'Does the name Ross Dolby mean anything to you, Miss Lessard?'

'The famous artist?'

He gave a dry chuckle. 'So you know he's an artist, and that he's famous. One of South Africa's greats as a matter of fact. Have you read anything about him? Seen any of his work?'

'I went to an exhibition a few months ago.'

'Liked what you saw?'

Kirby wrinkled her brow. 'Ross Dolby's work . . .' She was quiet a few moments as she tried to bring the pictures to mind. 'His paintings are bold and raw and innovative,' she said at last. 'I remember thinking that some people might not be comfortable having them hang on their walls.'

'Are you such a person?'

'Oh, no.' She gave him a smile that was at once open and appealing. 'I liked his work. It's not pretty-pretty, Mr Anderson, and I wish now that I'd paid more attention to the exhibition . . . But I know that I liked what I saw.'

'Ah.' Her boss looked satisfied. 'That's one hurdle over. Now I wonder if you'll like the man himself.'

Kirby stared at him, hope mingling with disbelief in the lovely green eyes. 'You mean . . . You want me to interview him?'

'More than that.' Hugh Anderson put down the pencil he was holding, and spread his hands on the desk. 'Miss Lessard, how would you like to ghost-write Ross Dolby's biography?'

The breath jerked in Kirby's throat. She had *dreamed* of just such an opportunity. 'I'd love it!'

'It wouldn't be easy,' warned her boss. 'Ross Dolby can be a temperamental man.'

'I'd have the patience of an angel,' she promised.

'It's possible that his hours wouldn't be regular.'

'I never clock-watch.'

'That's true, it's one of the things I've noticed about you. That, and the way you write.'

Kirby flushed with pleasure. She was a girl who collected bright moments. She kept them in a special part of her mind and took them out now and then, dusted them so to speak, as some people dust a collection of china. She meant to cherish Mr Anderson's praise.

'Let me tell you about the assignment.' He sat back in his chair. 'You know that we've been publishing a lot of biographies lately. Artists, musicians, sportsmen. People in the public eye.'

'Like Ross Dolby.'

'Precisely. He's quite a feather in our caps. Any number of publishing houses would have been delighted with the chance to put out his book. He chose to come to us.'

Don't thumb your nose at an opportunity, said a silent voice in Kirby's head. Opportunities had come her way so very sporadically since Meg's birth. As for an opportunity of this kind—it was so fantastic that she could hardly believe it was true.

And yet she had to ask the question. 'Why me, Mr Anderson?'

'I think you're the right person for it.'

'Sally, and Mrs Grant . . . They've had so much more experience . . .'

An eyebrow lifted. 'Don't you want the assignment, Miss Lessard?'

'Oh yes!'

Hugh Anderson smiled at her eagerness. 'Then go for it, Kirby.' He used her name for the first time since she'd known him. 'This book could well lead to others.' He paused. 'As to the why. I like your approach. It's fresh and unusual. Ross Dolby is an unusual man.'

Kirby felt a warm glow spreading through her. 'When do I start?'

'That's something you'll have to discuss with the man himself. I've told him to expect you around ten tomorrow morning.'

That was how sure her boss had been of her. But Kirby didn't mind. Her feet seemed not to be touching the ground at all as she left his office and walked back to her desk.

'It's the chance of a life-time, Lynn,' said Kirby late that afternoon. 'I still can't believe it.'

'It sounds fantastic.' Lynn was Meg's baby-sitter, and Kirby's best friend. 'When do you start?'

'I drive out to see Ross Dolby tomorrow morning.' Kirby's eyes went to the little girl who was playing with her doll in a corner of the room. 'Life is strange,' she said reflectively. 'That's a cliché, but it's true too. Three years ago I felt as if my world had ended. There I was, looking forward to university, and then I found I was pregnant. Oh, the havoc it caused.'

'You never talk about it,' Lynn said.

'Until recently I couldn't. I had to put all my strength just into surviving. Now ... Well, three years is a long time. I can look back at last.'

'You never mention the father.'

'He was a student. And reluctant to give up his chance of a profession.'

'He didn't try to help you?'

Kirby's lips twisted wryly. 'He wanted me to have an abortion.'

'And you said no . . .'

'Absolutely. A social worker suggested I give up the baby for adoption.' Her eyes softened as she watched Meg cuddling her doll. 'Can you imagine life without my Meg?'

'It hasn't been easy for you.'

'It was very hard, especially at the beginning. I wondered so often if I'd done the right thing. But I came through it.'

'With no regrets?' Lynn asked curiously.

'Not any more. Oh, I'd have liked a father for Meg. But not Jimmy. At the time when we . . . Well, I thought I loved him.'

Kirby was silent a few moments, eyes dark with memory. On a new note she continued. 'I'd planned to study too. To be an architect. But things worked out differently. I adore Meg, I find myself begrudging every minute I'm not with her.'

'And now you have a career too.'

'The beginnings of one anyway.' Kirby took a sip of her coffee. 'I keep thinking I'm dreaming. I still can't believe that I'll be ghost-writing a famous artist's biography.'

'Sounds as if you'll be very busy. Where's the time for a man in all this?'

Kirby put her mug down with unusual firmness. 'There isn't any. I don't want a man, Lynn. Never again. I'm finished with love. Or what passes for it.'

'You're only twenty-two.'

'Old enough to know what I want out of life. A satisfying career. To watch my darling Meg grow up, and to give her everything I can.' Kirby went over to her daughter, and began to gather up her toys. It was time to take Meg home.

'No men for me,' she said as she put the toys in a box. 'They only bring trouble. I'm going to make it on my own.'

It was a marvellous day to be taking the winding coastal road out of Cape Town. For once there was no mist on Table Mountain, and the Twelve Apostles, the range that stood like bastions behind the outlying suburbs of the city, were so clear that every niche on the rugged slopes seemed to be visible. So spectacular was the road—the mountains rising steeply on one side, the ocean incredibly blue on the other—that people often likened it to Italy's Amalfi Drive.

But as Kirby negotiated the bends, her mind was far away from the beauty all around her. She could only think of Ross Dolby. Who was he, this man who had become so famous in the art world? She'd thought of him last night, right up to the moment that she had drifted into sleep, and now she had a picture of him in her mind. A recluse living in a shack on the slope of the mountains. White shock of hair, craggy face with great sunken eyes. Long thin sensitive fingers, hands stained from years of working with oils.

He'd probably be the very opposite of what she imagined, she thought wryly. Small and neat and spry, adoring the grandchildren who played at his knee when he was not painting, living in a marvellous Cape Dutch house that was part gallery, part museum.

But the house, when she found it eventually, was neither a Cape Dutch museum nor a shack. Only its isolation—no houses for miles around—fitted in with what Kirby had imagined. It was a thoroughly modern house, built into the mountainside, layered and sloping with its slope. All big windows and rough brick, she saw, with a panoramic view over the ocean.

Her heart was beating faster than usual as she walked to the door and rang the bell. It began to thud very hard when the door was opened and a vital voice said, 'Miss Lessard?'

The man who stood looking at her was tall and broad-shouldered, his arms tanned and corded in the manner of one who spent much of his time out of doors. His hair was dark and untidy, as if the Cape wind had blown through it, and his jeans and the *veldskoene* on his feet were spattered with wet sand. But it was the eyes that held her attention. Beneath thick winging brows, they were dark and intent. Eyes that seemed to see deeper than other eyes. As if they stripped an object to its core—or a person to her soul, Kirby thought in sudden confusion.

To the girl whose credo it was to let no man hurt her or get to her ever again, the thought was not pleasant. Perhaps he was an assistant to the artist, she told herself.

She summoned her most professional voice and smile. 'Yes, I'm Kirby Lessard, and I've come to see Mr Dolby.'

'I'm Ross Dolby and I'm delighted to see you.'

She'd known it of course, even though she'd wished it otherwise. He put out his hand, and after a brief hesitation—how she cursed herself a moment later for that—she met it with her own hand. His grip was cool and firm, and it lasted just a few seconds. It didn't justify the quiver that ran up her arm.

Striving for composure, she followed him into a room that was all light and space, almost as if there were only windows and no walls. But there were walls of course, and on them hung paintings, two of which bore the signature of Ross Dolby. Kirby would have known them for his even without the name in the corner. Starkly bold and spare, there was a haunting quality in them which she recognised.

She was unable to look at them properly because he had stopped close beside her. 'Miss Lessard, I think I've surprised you in some way.' He was watching her.

She gave a rueful smile and took a step away, more comfortable with the extra space between them. 'You don't have white hair and a craggy face.'

His laugh was as vital as his voice. 'So you thought I'd be older. Come to think of it, you're also much younger than the person I was expecting. And do you make it a habit to keep honey-suckle in your hair?'

She looked at him, puzzled, and then he'd closed the space she had created, and she felt his fingers in her hair. They came away, holding a sprig of honey-suckle. 'You must have taken it with you as you came in through the door,' he said.

She managed to suppress a sudden breathlessness, so that her 'I expect so,' came out softly. She had to widen the space again, but this time she did it more skilfully, pretending an interest in a wooden carving that stood on a nearby table, taking two steps away from Ross Dolby so that she could see it.

'Done by Pierre Lautrail.' She heard the tinge of amusement in his tone.

Keeping flushed cheeks turned away from him, she said, 'It's very beautiful.'

'Beautiful,' he agreed drily, and she was glad he could not see her face. 'It's a perfect day, Miss Lessard, why don't we talk outside?'

He was so polite, so correct, this man who looked more like a fisherman than an artist. There was nothing to do but follow him again as he led the way out on to a patio that jutted away from the house, giving one the impression of being on a ship's deck on the Atlantic.

'Make yourself comfortable,' he said, gesturing to a chair. 'I'll be back in a moment.'

Kirby did not sit down. She walked instead to the edge of the patio, and watched the turbulence of the swell. Matching her mood, she thought with a frown. For things were not turning out as she'd imagined. Ross Dolby, far from being an old man, was too young, too good-looking. Sensitive and aesthetic he might be—had to be, she supposed— but the qualities were not obvious. Obvious were his looks and his vitality. And his sexuality. A rampant sexuality that seemed as much a part of the man as the lines of his rugged face and the dark hair on his head.

'You should see it at sunset.' She had not been aware of his return. 'You'll love it, Kirby.'

All her life she'd been called Kirby, and yet her name sounded odd on his lips. He came to stand beside her, so close that the hairs on his big arm brushed against her. He seemed not to share her problem with space. She was intensely aware of him, but this time she did not move away. He would be amused if she did. She could live with his closeness, she told herself as she made a decision, because she wouldn't be experiencing it again after today.

'It would be a marvellous view at sunset,' she said politely, without turning, and heard his burst of laughter.

'Are you always so prim, Kirby?'

She had not meant to look at him, but the question had her swinging round. The long-forgotten excitement that she had thought never to experience again, the awareness that made her conscious of every inch of his body and hers, owed nothing to primness. But it was important that he did not know how she felt. Better by far that he should think her prim and stand-offish. Good armour against a man who would be anything but prim himself.

She shrugged. 'I suppose so.'

He laughed again. 'Is that what you'd have the world think?'

He was so close to the mark that she was startled. Her face was still turned his way. As her eyes met his they were wide and green and vulnerable, and her lips were parted a little. And then she remembered who she was, and what she had determined to become, and her lashes came down, and she turned her head towards the ocean once more. Her heart was beating so hard that she could actually feel the separate beats against her rib-cage, and she wasn't helped by the closeness of a warm male body just inches from her own.

'I have a feeling you could do with some refreshment,' Ross said.

It was in fact just what she needed. A cup of coffee or a glass of fruit juice to settle her raw nerves. A chair to sit on. A few moments of sheer mundaneness in which to regain the composure she had come to value so dearly.

But it was a bottle of wine that stood on the weathered wooden table behind them. 'Wine?' she asked in surprise. 'At this time of the morning?'

'It's appropriate, don't you think?' Somehow he was bringing out the ninny in her, and she hated him for it.

He was laughing again, the deep laugh that seemed to come all the way from his shoes, and so easily. 'That's the prim Kirby speaking. Do you usually drink your toasts in tea?'

'Are we drinking a toast?'

'To joint ventures.'

She didn't like the sound of that 's'. Even one venture with Ross Dolby, however tempting—and God knew, it *was* tempting—might well be too many.

'To joint ventures,' he repeated when they were seated opposite each other, and he was raising his glass to her.

'Mr Dolby . . .'

'Ross. Do you expect me to bare my soul to a woman who calls me Mr Dolby?'

A roguish grin made him look devastating. 'You're not at all my idea of an artist.' They weren't the words she'd meant to say.

'You're not my idea of a ghost-writer.' His eyes were on hers.

It was her chance. 'Then I'm not the right one for the assignment.'

'I don't agree,' he said softly.

'I'm too prim for you.'

'I don't believe you're prim at all. You have marvellous eyes, did you know?' His teeth were white and wicked against his tan. 'There you go, pursing your lips at me. But your soul is in your eyes, Kirby, and I like what I see there.'

'Mr Dolby, I don't think . . .'

'Ross, and drink your wine.'

She did, and it was dry, and very good.

'Splendid,' he said. 'You've sealed the toast.'

To joint ventures. Even with the wine inside her, she was unhappy. 'Mr Dolby, I don't think . . .'

'*Ross,*' he insisted. 'Just keep remembering that I'm going to be baring my soul to you.' His eyes were on her again. 'And you'll bare yours to me.'

'That's not part of the arrangement,' she burst out.

'To me it is. If I know you, I can talk to you, and if I can talk to you it might be a good book.'

It really could be a good book. Ross Dolby was no ordinary man. People would want to read about him. The writer in Kirby yearned to write about him.

But there was the man himself, and the effect he was having on her. The woman in Kirby, who had been hurt, who had decided never to be hurt again, knew she had to escape. When she got back to the office she would ask Mr Anderson to relieve her of the assignment. There were others who would give all they had for the chance to work with Ross Dolby.

'Bring your things with you when you come,' he said. 'Be sure to bring along slacks and a couple of warm sweaters—it can get cold here at night.'

'Night?' She stared at him, forgetting for the moment that she would not be coming at all. 'I'd be going back to Cape Town each day.'

'Wrong.' There was a gleam in the dark eyes. 'You'd be staying here.'

She was confused. 'But why? Once you'd

finished dictating there'd be no reason for me to
stay. I'd be doing the actual writing at home.'

His eyes went over her, and she had the
strangest feeling that he saw beneath the clothes
she wore to the essential Kirby Lessard. Men had
undressed her with their eyes before now—it was
not a new experience for a reasonably attractive
girl. But she had never had the feeling that a man
was seeing through the skin and the bones to the
very depths of her being.

'If we're going to work together we should
understand each other,' Ross said. 'And the first
thing to understand is that this is not going to be
a nine-to-five job. I won't be sitting down with you
in my little study each day, at a set hour, to dictate
the story of my life.'

Despite her decision not to sit with him at all,
she was nevertheless fascinated. 'What is your
method of working then?'

'I don't keep set hours. I work when the mood
takes me. There will be days when I will want to
paint, when I'll be grouchy and won't feel like
talking to you. And there will be other days when
I won't stop.'

'I see,' she said cautiously.

'There will be times when I function best in the
mornings, other times when we'll talk best at night.'

'At night?'

'At night,' he repeated, with that gleam in his
eyes. 'There it is again. The primness. You
wouldn't be frightened to stay in the house with
me, would you, Kirby?'

'Of course not,' she said, but she was lying.

Yes, she would be frightened. She was already
frightened of this big handsome man. Frightened
of the sexuality which she sensed in him rather

than saw. Frightened of her own reactions to him.

Jimmy had been a lesson to her. She had resolved never to allow herself to be in a man's power again. And for three years she had been successful. There were men who asked her out, but put off by her aloofness there was seldom a second invitation. To Kirby's complete satisfaction. Men had no place in her life. Meg and making a career for herself, those were the only things that mattered to her now.

Though the wine was good, she drank sparingly, mindful of the winding road back to Cape Town. Ross Dolby had no such considerations. She watched him drink his wine. He seemed to savour every golden drop. He was a man who would savour life, she thought. The kind of man who would walk right into life, zestfully and unafraid, enjoying the good to the fullest, riding the bad with some profound philosophy that was uniquely his own.

I'm playing psychiatrist she thought, and wondered at herself, for she had long made it a point to remain uninvolved with the men she met, not only socially and physically, but on an emotional level as well. Yet there was something about this man which seemed to defy uninvolvement. Something earthy, of the earth. An attractive quality, immensely appealing. Which was why he was so dangerous.

'Like the wine?' he asked.

'Delicious.'

'Spoken in the same way you'd express your opinion on a decent piece of steak. You intrigue me, Kirby Lessard.'

'Why?' She met his gaze, but the hand that held the glass was not quite steady.

'Because your manner, your words, are at variance with what I read in you.'

'I'm not one of your models, Mr Dolby.' Her voice shook.

'You will be,' he said softly, letting the irritating use of his last name pass.

He lifted his glass to his lips again, as if in a new toast—a toast to what? She looked at the hand that held the glass. It was broad and strong, the fingers long and square and rather flat-edged. She tried to imagine that hand holding a paintbrush, and failed. She imagined it caressing her skin—and shoved the picture from her mind.

'I really must be going,' she said.

'We'll start on Monday,' he suggested.

'We haven't established that I'm going to be starting at all.'

'Why don't you come around ten? That seems to be a time that suits us both.'

'I don't think you understand, Mr Dolby.'

'Ross. And remember to bring some casual wear. You won't be needing much in the way of suits and dresses.'

'You can discuss clothing with whoever does come.'

He looked at her so intently, and for such a long time, that she started to tremble. At last he said, 'What made you so scared of life?'

'I'm *not* scared.' Said with defiance.

'Life is fun, Kirby. When you allow it to be.'

The pronouncement shouldn't have shaken her. But it did. When was the last time she'd allowed life to be fun? In a time long past, existing in another world. She stared at him a moment, into eyes that were deep and brown and much too far-seeing. No amusement in them now. But there was an expression all the same, and Kirby understood quite suddenly what it was. Compassion.

She stood up abruptly, her hand hitting against the wine-glass, catching it in the moment that it would have fallen.

'I must go.' Blindly she stepped away from the table, and a low voice said, 'This way,' and a hand cupped her elbow and guided her in the right direction.

He kept his hand on her arm as they walked through the big glass doors into the living-room, and Kirby was aware of each finger on her skin. Disturbingly aware. Achingly. God help me, she thought, what's happened to my strength of will? To my resolve never to feel again?

'Goodbye, Mr Dolby.' Her face and her voice were controlled as she parted from him at the door of her car. But inwardly she was shaking. She was still shaking when she drove away from the house on the cliff and took the road back to Cape Town.

Mr Anderson was surprisingly unyielding when she told him of her decision not to ghost-write Ross Dolby's biography.

'I want you to do it.'

'I can't.' Her look of pleading should have melted the heart of a sterner man.

'You will.'

'There must be someone else. Sally is almost done with her current assignment.'

'Yesterday,' said the new Mr Anderson whom she did not recognise, 'this was the chance of a life-time.'

'Yes . . .'

'It's the *only* chance,' he said. He did not elaborate. He did not need to. Kirby understood what he meant.

*　　*　　*

Lynn stared at her incredulously, when Kirby asked her to look after Meg. 'What changed your mind?'

'The man himself.'

'He's an ogre?'

'Anything but.'

'Well then?'

'I thought he'd be old and sunken. A creative hermit. He's young, Lynn, mid-thirties I'd say. Good-looking, and so attractive.'

'Either I'm crazy or you are,' her friend said feelingly. 'What's wrong about working for a young good-looking genius?'

'It's the way he made me feel.'

A look of understanding came suddenly into Lynn's eyes. 'He made a pass at you?'

Kirby got restlessly to her feet, and went to stand at the window. The building was on the slope of Table Mountain with a view over the suburbs and the city to the docks. It was dark, and here and there lights were beginning to appear. Kirby's inner shaking had long vanished. Now there was a rigidity that made her neck and shoulders a solid mass of tension.

'He did make a pass at you.' Lynn's voice came from behind her.

'No. A pass I could have dealt with. What he did was make me feel like a woman.'

'Is that so bad?'

'To me it is.' Kirby spun round. 'Remember what I told you yesterday? That no man would ever hurt me again?'

'You say he didn't touch you,' Lynn said uncertainly.

'Not physically. He touched me in a way that was much worse. I was aware of him as a man. Of myself as a woman.'

'He's sexy then?'

'He's sexual. There's a difference, Lynn. He's the most sexual man I ever met.'

'You . . . you wanted him to make love to you?' The uncertainty was still present in Lynn's voice. Close as they were, there were things one did not discuss with Kirby.

'No! And yet . . .' Her voice shook. 'I wondered what it would be like. He touched my elbow, oh, in the most courteous way, and I felt . . .' She sounded suddenly fierce. 'I don't want to think about it.'

'You're frightened,' Lynn said gently.

'That's what he said, and I denied it. Lynn, I'm terrified.'

'You don't think he'd . . . well, do anything to you?'

'Not for a moment. Lynn, I felt vulnerable. And I want so much to be strong. I've set my goals and I mean to achieve them. Sex has no place in my life.'

'What about love?' Lynn asked softly.

'Who's talking love?' Kirby responded shortly.

Neither girl spoke for a while. In an arm-chair, oblivious of the strained silence that had fallen between her mother and her baby-sitter, little Meg lay sleeping.

At length Lynn said, 'So you've rejected the assignment.'

'I've accepted it. My boss gave me no alternative. In fact he made the options quite clear. No Ross Dolby book, no chance of anything else.'

'Did he give you a reason?'

'No, but he was adamant.' Kirby frowned. 'It was really quite strange.'

'What are you going to do? I mean you feel so

strongly about the man.'

Kirby looked at her. 'I feel just as strongly about my career. This assignment could lead to others. It's what I've wanted for so long. I have to make it, Lynn, for Meg's sake, and for my own.'

CHAPTER TWO

HE was in the garden, squatting on the ground when she arrived. Dressed in shabby jeans and a faded T-shirt, he was surrounded by a tumble of fishing-nets.

'Mr Dolby,' she said, and he looked up and saw her, and his face broke into a roguish grin. She'd spent the weekend hoping he wasn't really so very good-looking, but her hopes had been unfounded—he was even more attractive than she'd remembered him.

'Hello, Kirby. Ten o'clock on the dot. I should have known you'd be punctual.'

'Punctuality is part of being professional,' she said, and felt a little stupid.

'So it is,' he agreed cheerfully. 'And the expression on your face tells me that the sight of an artist mending fishing-nets when he should be catching the best of the morning light makes you think he is thoroughly unprofessional—or a little crazy.'

He was baiting her, just as he'd baited her the first time she'd met him. And so instead of saying politely, 'Oh no, not at all,' she smiled and said, 'Perhaps a little of both.'

And what would Mr Anderson make of such heresy? Remembering the way her boss had turned stubborn when he'd seen that she did not want the assignment, she felt some satisfaction in the knowledge that she didn't care.

Ross chuckled, apparently unruffled by her

answer. 'What luggage have you brought with you?'

'A suitcase and a light bag.'

'I'll bring the case in for you later. Why don't you take the bag and go into the house? Your room is the second on the right after the living-room. I'll wait for you out here.'

'We'll start work then?'

Dark eyes held a wicked gleam. 'I hope so. Not in those clothes though. Are you able to reach something less formal?'

It really had nothing to do with him what she wore, but she said, 'Probably.'

'Good. See you out here then.'

He *was* crazy she decided. A craziness that did not detract in the least from the sexuality and attractiveness she had glimpsed the first time. Or perhaps enhanced it. Ross Dolby was the most attractive man she had ever met—certainly more attractive than Jimmy. Which was why she'd probably been crazy herself to take on the assignment. Her career notwithstanding.

She found the second door to the right and opened it. Took a few steps inside. And stopped in astonishment. She had given no thought to the room she would be sleeping in for the next weeks, but had she done so only a few of the things she saw now would have been as she imagined them. The lovely antique chest of drawers, made of stinkwood and intricately carved. The Cape Dutch wardrobe. A graceful riempie-chair, the hide thongs looking as if they had been well cared for.

There were two paintings. One was a Pierneef. An original? She had never seen an original Pierneef outside a gallery, but instinct told her she was looking at one of the master's works now. The other painting was a Ross Dolby. There were the raw colours, the strong lines, the throbbing vitality she had come to associate with the man she was going to be working with.

But the rest of the room was a surprise. The floor was made of yellow-wood, the kind of floor Kirby had seen in museums, always covered in priceless carpets that were either Chinese or Persian. On this floor there was a roughly-woven rather lovely Basuto mat in muted tones of rust and beige. The bed was a four-poster, Louis the Fourteenth, Kirby guessed. On it was a patch-work spread, very pretty but incongruously modern. In the niche of a bay-window that gave on to one of those incredible views of the sea, was a small table, modern too, and on it stood a vase filled with wild flowers. There was nothing careful or elaborate about the arrangement. Rather it was as if Ross Dolby had gone walking on the mountain slopes earlier that morning, had picked flowers as he saw them, and had thrust them in the vase just as they'd been held in his hand. There were two other paintings on the walls, both abstracts executed by artists whose names Kirby had never heard. One was a series of dots and circles, the other a merging welter of lines. They meant nothing to her, but she had to admit that she liked them.

Altogether it was the strangest combination of things in one room that she had even seen. If she had hoped to get some clues to Mr Dolby's personality by the way he furnished his house, then she was more confused now than she had been before.

A bathroom led from the bedroom, and she stepped inside to look round there too. The bath-

tub was antique and elegant, a piece that would
have looked quite at home in an old Cape Dutch
house open for viewing to the public. But the rest
of the fittings were thoroughly modern. Even on
these walls there were pictures, and here too was
the mix she had seen in the bedroom. A
nineteenth-century vase of flowers and a charcoal-
penned scene of urchins playing in a city street
hung side by side.

Already she had some material for the book she
would write. Whether Ross Dolby knew it or not,
Kirby thought his many admirers would be
interested in this unusual side of the man whose
paintings were sold for such huge sums.

Change into something less formal, he'd said,
and she decided to humour him. Cool and
professional she would be, but there was no point
in antagonising the man even before they started
working together. Fortunately a pair of trousers
and a shirt were within easy reach.

She went back into the bedroom, and for the
first time she saw the piece of paper that lay at the
pillowed end of the bed. A note? Surely not.
Curiously she picked it up.

And drew in her breath. A pencilled picture. A
portrait. With that familiar sprawling signature
beneath it. A face she recognised. Herself. Kirby
Lessard, with her hair in a neat chignon, and a
small frown between her eyes, and her lips just
slightly parted as if she had been about to say
something and thought better of it.

Kirby looked at the picture for a least a minute.
The expression on her face was one she recognised,
she'd seen it herself sometimes. It was not the
expression that met her eyes when she put on her
make-up or when she checked her appearance. But

she'd seen it sometimes unexpectedly, when she'd found herself looking into a mirror without meaning to. This was the Kirby that Lynn would have seen when they'd discussed Ross Dolby. Friday. The Kirby Mr Anderson would have recognised as being the girl who had asked to be released from the assignment. The Kirby Ross Dolby had seen a few days ago, when she'd found herself questioning the wisdom of working with him.

The astounding thing was that he had caught the expression so well that he had been able to sketch it from memory. He was a perceptive man, no doubt about that. Too perceptive. The frown in the sketch was between her eyes at the moment, she could feel it. She would have to be on her guard with him. Every morning, before she got out of the four-poster bed, she would remind herself to be careful.

A final look, and then she put the portrait down. A signed Ross Dolby. Not an oil or a water-colour, but a Ross Dolby all the same. Even a squiggle with his signature would have to be worth something. Did famous artists make a habit of giving their work away so casually? She wouldn't have thought so. But perhaps, rather unbelievably, a quickly-pencilled sketch given freely to a girl he hardly knew meant as little to the man as the sun that was even now moving to its zenith while the artist repaired a fishing-net, uncaring of the precious hours of light that he was wasting.

He was still busy with the net when she came outside, notebook and pencil in hand. He looked up, and his eyes went over her figure, trim in well-cut cords and a tailored lemon shirt, and the expression in his face was so thoroughly male and assessing that she felt herself stiffen.

'You'd look even nicer with your hair loose,' he told her.

Something quivered along her spine. 'I like my hair this way.'

'Because it makes you look remote?'

He was so close to the mark, this man, that she felt dangerously vulnerable. 'I don't think that concerns you, Mr Dolby.'

His hand reached out without warning, seizing a slender wrist. 'Ross,' he said.

After a moment she said, 'Ross . . .' The sound of his name on her lips was infinitely less disturbing than the pressure of his fingers on her soft skin. It was really absurd, yet she felt as if her wrist was on fire.

'Ah . . .' He said it softly, and released her wrist. 'You'll remember my name from now on, will you, Kirby?'

She shrugged. Really, it was extraordinarily hard to know how to behave with him. Here she was, notebook and pencil at the ready to start working, and he seemed bent on shattering her composure.

'So you want to look remote,' he said.

'I didn't say that.'

'No, you very politely told me the matter was not my concern.'

She lifted her chin, stung by his tone. 'It isn't.' And she was conscious too late that by the very intensity of her response she had dented, if only for a moment, her precious armour against him.

His eyes gleamed. 'I do know that it's important to you, that remoteness of yours.' He paused, and she thought he had said as much as he meant to say. But he went on. 'In time you'll tell me why.'

Not 'perhaps'. Or 'you may want to tell me'.

Just a statement of fact. Oh, but he was a self-assured fellow, this artist who did not have the look of an artist. So handsome in a rugged earthy way, so physically appealing. Nothing remote or cool about him. On the contrary, he seemed infinitely warm and approachable. A man who was satisfied to let the world see him just as he was, without mask or façade. But then Kirby did not believe that Ross Dolby was a man who needed a mask, that he'd ever known such a need. His self-assurance was such that it was almost a kind of arrogance.

And she wondered how in so short a time she could know so much about him.

Letting her lashes fall across her eyes because it had become too difficult to meet his gaze, she opened her notebook. 'I'm ready to begin.' Her voice was cool.

'You won't be needing that book.'

'I won't? Not today you mean?'

'Never.'

She looked at him startled. He was watching her, and she saw that his expression was amused. But there was understanding too, and that disturbed her far more than the amusement. She did not want Ross to understand her. It was the one thing she did not want.

'I don't understand,' she said. 'I thought you'd be dictating your life-story.'

'I'll be telling it to you. There's a difference.'

If there was, she failed to see it. 'But I'll still be taking notes,' she said after a moment. 'I'll be basing the book on them.'

That was her understanding of the way the book would be written. Perhaps his ideas were different. If so, it would be best to clarify the matter at the start.

'Right,' Ross said. 'But you won't be taking notes on paper.'

She was puzzled. 'What other way is there?'

'You'll imprint what I say on your brain. We'll talk, you and I, and you'll get as much material as you want. You've only to ask. And then you can write your book.'

'No written notes at all?' she asked after a long moment, when she'd had a chance to think over what he'd said.

'None at all. I can't stand the sight of a notebook and pencil.'

It wasn't the way the other writers at Anderson's worked. She'd seen them come into the office, piles of notes in hand. Had seen the professional books they turned out.

'It's the way people work,' she said doubtfully.

'It may be how other ghost-writers work. People who've become used to certain conditions. But you've come to this project with a fresh mind.'

She stared at him, her eyes green and wide and confused. 'You know this is my first time as a ghost-writer?' She was unaware that for a moment the remoteness was missing.

'It's the way I wanted it.'

'So that's why . . .'

Why Mr Anderson had chosen her for the assignment. There was a taste of bitterness in her mouth. Which she thrust from her. No matter why he'd chosen her, or that she felt suddenly a little disappointed and cheated. What counted was that she had the opportunity to work with Ross Dolby, and that if she made a success of the book it might lead to other things.

'Don't think I'm not professional,' she said. And the way she said it made it sound like a challenge.

He smiled. 'Of course you are.'

His smile was not merely a matter of lips parting to reveal teeth that were strong and white against his tan. It was a smile which reached his eyes, warming them, giving his face an extra vitality. She wondered what it would be like to be kissed by him. It was not the first time the thought had occurred to her, and as involuntarily. Appalled and angry, she pushed the picture—an unexpectedly tempting picture—from her.

Putting down the notebook, she said, 'Well, I'm ready to begin.'

'Do you know how to fix a fishing-net?' he asked.

'No. Mr Dolby, I said I'm ready to . . .'

'Ross,' he cut in mildly. 'Come here, Kirby, come sit by me and let me show you.'

He was joking, she thought at first. He had to be. But a look at his face showed that he was serious. Fishing-nets were on his mind today. And geniuses, she'd gathered, were hard people to argue with.

So after a moment she kneeled down beside him.

'Like this,' he said, gathering the skeins where the netting was broken, and sewing them together with a long needle. 'And like this, Kirby. Are you watching?'

She was watching. But she was watching his hands as much as the way he fixed the net. Such strong hands, tanned and broad-fingered. She had been fascinated by them the first day, and she was fascinated again now. The sight of those hands drew her like magnets, keeping her eyes on them, defying them to move away.

'Nothing to it, is there?' he asked.

'Nothing.'

'Feel up to trying it?'

'Why not.'

'Good.'

He smiled again, and her heart did a funny movement against her rib-cage. He was so close to her that she was aware of every inch of the long body, muscled and sinewed and powerful. Too aware. She did not like the sensations she felt starting inside her. She was done with that kind of thing. Everyone was entitled to make mistakes, but she'd made hers, and she was not going to make them again. She'd made up her mind that she was never going to be stirred by a man again, and she was not about to let this dynamic self-assured artist affect her.

Yet the smile did strange things to her nonetheless. She hadn't realised that there were flecks in the dark irises of his eyes, or that the smile warmed them and turned the flecks to gold. She hadn't bargained on the way the smile would make her feel—filling her with a strange and aching longing that she couldn't—wouldn't—put a name to.

So it was a relief to be able to move a little away from him. 'Sure I'd like to try,' she said. 'Give me a net.'

'We'll work on this one together.'

'Together?' Again the movement of her heart in her chest.

'It's really quite easy,' he said, looking amused, as if he sensed her embarrassment. He threw a portion of his net across to her, letting it fall on her lap. She picked up the needle he gave her, and bent her head, glad of the chance to look away from him. She must have absorbed something of what he'd shown her, for after an awkward start she was able to mend a rip.

'Splendid.' The voice that came to her across the small space that separated them was deep and vital. 'Comfortable where you are?'

'Yes,' she lied. Actually she was feeling distinctly uncomfortable. The fishing-net, stretching from his lap to hers, created an intimacy that bothered her.

'I really thought we were going to do some work this morning,' she said at last. 'Isn't that why you told me to come here today?'

'You don't call this work?'

'I thought you'd be dictating.'

'I don't dictate,' Ross said. 'I talk. I've explained that.' He grinned at her, and she felt weak despite her resolve. 'We're both going to be talking, you and I, at least at the beginning.'

'But the fishing-nets . . .'

'When the hands are busy it's sometimes easier to talk.'

She couldn't quarrel with that statement. Working with her hands gave her the excuse to look down at the net, away from those too-perceptive eyes. She wondered if Ross meant to conduct all their sessions this way. She would soon find out.

'Do you like your room?' he asked.

'Very much.'

'But?'

'How did you know there was a but?'

His lips were tilted at the corners. 'I can see it in your eyes.'

She couldn't help laughing back at him. 'You're a disconcerting man, Mr Dolby—Ross. Perhaps I should wear dark glasses.'

'Don't you dare,' he said equably. 'It would be a crime to hide such beautiful eyes. Now tell me about the but.'

'All right. It's such a mixture of periods.' She looked at him, and saw by his expression that he was listening to her. 'Cape Dutch furniture and a Louis the Fourteenth bed. That gorgeous yellow-wood floor with that rug. It's a lovely rug, in any other setting it would be perfect, but . . .'

'You think a Persian carpet would be more appropriate.'

'Well, yes. And the pictures. The Pierneef and your own work—hung with those abstracts . . .'

'The mixture offends you?'

He was putting her on the spot. 'It doesn't offend me. I just find it strange.'

'Why?' he asked softly. 'Do you feel there has to be method in all things, Kirby?'

Not half an hour in his company, and already he was making her question her values. Was this how it would be all the time?

'No,' she said. 'Not at all.'

'The but is still there.'

No getting off easily with Ross Dolby. Would she always have to watch every expression on her face, every word that she said?

'I've never seen a room like it,' she said carefully.

The tanned hands were busy with the net, but the dark eyes were on her face. 'Where is it written that a room must be all of one period, Kirby?'

'Nowhere. It just seems right.'

'Right to whom?'

She was beginning to feel trapped. 'I only know that you wouldn't find Cape Dutch furniture with a modern rug in a museum. There . . . there's no order in it.'

Ross said, 'There doesn't need to be order in all things. Sometimes disorder creates beauty. Your face is not symmetrical, Kirby, did you know that? But it's very beautiful in my eyes.'

The compliment disturbed her. She did not want compliments from this man. She shifted the net from one hand to the other.

She was relieved when he said, 'Just tell me one thing. Do you like the room?'

'I love it! It's a marvellous room.'

'I'm glad,' he said, and the strange thing was that he sounded as if he really meant it.

For a while they worked in silence, the small pale hands, the large tanned ones, close together, busy on the same net. At length Kirby said, 'I saw the picture.'

'So you found it.'

She looked at him. 'Is that the way you see me?'

'I wondered if you'd ask that.'

'Well, is it?'

'It's the image you've presented until now, isn't it? Conscientious, a bit worried about working with a madcap artist. A bit concerned at the fact that we are fixing a fishing-net and talking about your room and your face when we should be discussing the details of my life.'

'Is there anything wrong with that?' she asked defensively, a part of her wishing that he didn't see her that way, yet knowing it was better that he did.

'You asked me how I see you. Well, that picture shows the prim Kirby. She's the girl I chose to draw today.'

The way he said 'that picture' and 'today' made it sound as if he would draw her again.

'She's not the only Kirby I see.'

'Mr Dolby . . .'

'Still being prim, are you?' Surprisingly, he did not look annoyed. 'I think there's another Kirby, and she's not prim at all.'

He was so close to the truth, and after so short a time, that she felt frightened.

'I'm here to find out about you,' she said abruptly. 'Not the other way around. So why don't we stop talking about me, Mr Dolby ... Ross.'

'There's something you must understand,' he said gently. 'If we're going to work together there has to be a rapport. A sense of harmony.'

'I really don't think I'm the right person for you.' Her voice was jerky.

'I think you're ideal.' He said that so strangely. For a moment she had the oddest sensation, she felt quite light-headed.

'You want to know so much . . .'

'Only so that we can work together.' He touched her cheek, feather-lightly, and she had to sit very still to keep herself from flinching. 'As it is, I think I know quite a lot already.'

'I don't see how that's possible.'

'I think that you're trying very hard to be an independent career-woman. I know that you like order—and yet you enjoy disorder.'

'Mr Dolby . . .'

'And I think that behind that cool exterior there's a sadness and a wildness.'

This was too much. She got up abruptly, the net tumbling from her lap. 'Let's go on another time.'

'Have I touched you on the raw? I'm sorry.' There was an unnerving gentleness in the apology. 'All right, Kirby. Let's talk about me. Sit down again. That's right . . .'

And then he asked, 'Have you formed an opinion of me?'

CHAPTER THREE

KIRBY looked beyond the patio over the rolling blue waves of the Atlantic. Society had already given its opinion of Ross Dolby. He was a genius. A brilliant artist whose name would live for ever in the annals of South African art. Of world art perhaps. Eminent critics had given their opinion. The first night of any exhibition of Ross Dolby's work was a social event, and the plaudits that appeared in the press next day were unfailingly extravagant.

What could she possibly add to what had already been said?

'I want to know what *you* think of me.'

'You're a wonderful artist.'

'Don't repeat what you've heard.'

'I . . .'

'Or what you think I might want to hear.'

There was the hint of a smile in the rugged face with the laughter lines around the eyes and the mouth. He knew how difficult this was for her, Kirby realised suddenly.

'You really want me to be honest,' she said slowly.

'I wouldn't ask otherwise.'

'All right then.' She took a breath. 'I find it hard to think of you as an artist.'

And now what would he say? Sometimes people thought they wanted honesty when in fact they didn't want it at all.

He laughed delightedly. 'Why?'

'Because you're so totally out of character. Your hands, your face . . .'

His eyes gleamed. 'Don't stop.'

She'd said this much, she might as well say the rest. But he might not want to work with her when she'd said it, and she'd be sorry because she'd wanted so much to do this book.

'I can take it, you know,' he said, and she realised that he understood her thoughts.

And if that were the case, then perhaps she was being a darned fool even to consider going on with the assignment. The possibility of another book coming her way might not be worth the harm this man could do her. Because he *could* harm her. He was far more dangerous than Jimmy had ever been.

She lifted her chin in a challenge that even he would not be able to understand because it had nothing at all to do with what they were talking about. 'There's nothing sensitive or aesthetic about your appearance. Artists should be pale and haggard.'

'Should they?'

'At least that's the way the world thinks of you as a breed.'

'The world has been known to be wrong.'

'Yes . . .'

'Go on, Kirby. I don't believe you've finished.'

'It's not just that you're not pale. In fact, that's a ridiculous observation now that I think of it. But if you were a stranger, if I'd never met you before and didn't know who you were, I wouldn't take you for an artist. I'd think you had some outdoor occupation.'

'Such as?'

'A fisherman,' she said, remembering her earlier impression of him.

He laughed, delighted once more.

'Or an explorer,' Kirby went on. 'Perhaps the captain of a ship. Something like that.'

In a different era she might have taken him for a pirate, as much a looter of men's ships as of women's hearts, she thought, but did not say the thought aloud.

'Your fingers—they're wide and rough and broad. They look at home on this fishing-net. I can't picture them holding a paint-brush.'

'Excellent!'

She didn't know what to make of the response, but the dare-devil expression that had come into his eyes prompted her to go on. He really was an extraordinarily attractive man. Just as well she wasn't interested in him, for otherwise working with him, living with him in this magnificent isolation, could be disastrous to her peace of mind. Women must have been after Ross Dolby since he was old enough to hold a paint-brush, she imagined he could have any beautiful wealthy woman he wanted. He wouldn't remember the ghost-writer who would disappear from his life when the last word of the book had been written.

'Even the way you furnish your house.' She looked at him, saw the lifting of his lips at the corners, and said, 'I realise you don't like order, but wouldn't an artist *want* a rightness in things?'

'Not necessarily.'

'I've offended you, haven't I?' she asked.

'Would you care if you had?'

'Only because I really want the chance to do this book.'

This isn't happening, she thought. I'm not really saying these things to Ross Dolby. Mr Anderson would fire me on the spot if he knew.

'You're marvellous, do you know?' Incredibly, his eyes were sparkling.

'I am?' she asked doubtfully.

'For the last few minutes I haven't seen a trace of the prim Kirby Lessard.'

She looked at him in dismay. She hadn't meant to let down her guard. It was just . . . He'd drawn her out, she supposed. And that wasn't true either, she'd *allowed* him to draw her out.

'The frown is back between your eyebrows,' he said.

'I know, I can feel it.'

'It wasn't there while you were assessing me.'

'Mr Dolby . . .'

'Ross.' He took one of her hands in his, folding the fingers over so that they lay in his roughened palm. 'You didn't do anything wrong, you know.'

'I suppose not.'

'I asked you to be honest.'

He couldn't know that she had violated her own code, not his. She'd decided to remain on her guard with him, and in just a morning she'd found herself relaxing.

This was going to be some assignment.

'Please go on,' he said.

The hand that held hers was having an effect on her. It was so big and warm, and it seemed to communicate its warmness not only to her hand but to her wrist and her arm and the top of her spine. No! she thought.

She sat quite still for a moment, and then she pulled her hand away.

'That made you uncomfortable, did it?' he asked.

'Yes,' she said shortly.

'Why?'

Oh no, she thought, not again. 'We were talking about you,' she said sweetly.

After a moment he said, 'So we were. We've established that I couldn't possibly be an artist.'

For the first time she laughed. 'But you are one. A very famous one. That's why I'm here.'

'You're a perceptive girl. I think you're also a little confused.'

There was something inordinately appealing about him. Damn Jimmy. He'd made her distrust all men. Made her realise that men were not for her. But if Jimmy had never happened—how would she feel about Ross Dolby then?

'I am confused,' she admitted. 'I think you're a puzzle, Ross, and I think our readers are going to want to know about you.'

'You just called me by my name willingly for the first time.'

The conversation was becoming personal again. 'The readers are going to want to know about you,' she said again, steering the talk to safety. 'More so than if you were really the shrunken white-haired hermit of my imagination.'

'You'll tell them I'm a repairer of fishing-nets and a fraud.'

'The outdoor man's not the only side of you,' she said, knowing he was baiting her, and refusing to rise to it. 'I've seen your work. You're a wonderful artist. Sensitive. Creative.'

'You're quoting the critics again.'

'Yes . . . But not entirely. I've seen your work, Ross. In the galleries. In some of the big buildings. I know that what the critics say is true.'

'I think you're trying to say I'm a contradiction,' he said.

After a moment she said, 'That's true.'

'What about you?' The hand that had held hers reached out to cup her chin. 'Aren't you a contradiction too?'

His palm was rough beneath the soft skin of her chin, and his fingers lay on the side of her face. She could feel every one of them, knew just where they rested. There was nothing remotely lover-like in the touch, she knew that, and yet her body was responding just as if she was being caressed by a lover. Sensations that she had last felt three years ago were beginning to resurface. She was frightened. Very frightened.

'Remove your hand,' she said, calmly.

'There it is. The contradiction. Outwardly you're so cool, so remote. It's not only the words that say "don't touch".'

'It's the way I am.'

'I see another side.'

'Please, Ross . . .'

'Please, Ross. Don't go on touching me, that's what you're trying to say. Some women say "Please, Ross" in just that tone when they want me to make love to them.'

'I would never ask you that,' she gritted.

But just for a few seconds, the time it took to push the picture from her mind, she could actually see, feel, him making love to her. There was a sudden warmth in her loins. Her cheeks flushed, and without thinking what her actions might reveal, she dropped the net and put her hands to her face.

'No, you wouldn't ask.' His voice was very soft now. 'And yet the contradiction is there, Kirby. I can see the other side of the ice-maiden. I can see a girl who's wild and warm and passionate.'

'You're quite wrong.' After that moment of

weakness she had taken her hands away from her face and was facing him with all the coolness she could muster.

'That's what you'd like me to believe.' His hand was still beneath her chin, and now, with his thumb, he began a slow stroking movement downwards, along the sensitive skin of her throat. It was a gentle movement, but it was almost unbearably erotic.

'I wish you wouldn't do that,' Kirby said brittly. 'And you're really quite wrong about me. I look the way I am.'

'Some men might believe that.' His voice was still soft, but there was also a huskiness that she had not noticed before. 'But I'm an artist, Kirby, not only a man who repairs fishing-nets. I've trained myself to see behind the masks. I have to, if I only painted flat surfaces my work would be one-dimensional and not worthy of comment.'

She wished she knew what to say to that. With Jimmy she had been a very naive and innocent nineteen-year-old. She'd fallen for his talk of love, just as she had been overcome by the demands of her own body. Jimmy had been a lesson, a painful one in many ways, but worthwhile too because she could no longer imagine life without her little Meg. But he had been a lesson she was determined not to repeat. The men who asked her for dates soon learned that Kirby Lessard was a person who knew her own mind, who meant no when she said it. They did not persist with sexy conversation or demands—they learned quickly that they got nowhere with those. Till now she had been successful in freezing away the men who bothered her. It did not matter to her that she would not see them again—she did not want to.

Ross Dolby fell in a different category. She did not want to freeze him, her future career depended on working with him, on turning out a successful book about his life. But her privacy was very important to her. Her ice-maiden mask—and it was a mask, she knew that—had fooled every other man. It did not fool Ross. And she did not know what to do about it.

The next few weeks might be more difficult than she had ever anticipated. Over the years she had developed a few tricks in dealing with men, and up till now they had worked. Those tricks might not work with Ross. So relaxed on the surface, he was a determined man, persuasive too probably. What he wanted to know he would make a point of knowing.

But one thing he would never know, she vowed. She would never tell him about Meg.

Her nerves were at tearing-point when he took his hand from her face. 'Time for lunch,' he said with a kind of lop-sided grin. 'Hungry?'

'I could do with something to eat.'

It was a little early for lunch, but perhaps he realised that a break was called for. Sensitive he must be, at least in some respects.

'Why don't you stay out here?' he suggested. 'It won't take me long to prepare.'

She could have offered to help him, she supposed, but she didn't. A few minutes quite alone, without Ross Dolby, was what she needed. Standing up, she stretched her cramped legs and walked to the edge of the patio. It was a glorious day. The sea was intensely blue and the sky was cloudless. On this wild stretch of coast there was little habitation for miles on either side. Below her she saw a beach, pretty but deserted, and Kirby knew why. The beaches on False Bay on the other side of the peninsula were crowded most days of the week, for the Indian Ocean was so warm that its waves were beloved by surfers and swimmers. Not so the Atlantic. Intrepid was the soul who ventured into the icy depths of these waters.

Despite the fact that Kirby loved to swim, for sheer beauty this was the side of the peninsula she liked best. There was something about the strong sea, the rugged mountains, the rocky beaches, that appealed to the wild part of her nature which Ross, perceptive Ross, had glimpsed. Perhaps because the wildness was echoed in his own nature. The thought brought her up with a start. They had nothing in common, she and Ross Dolby. And yet if she could choose one site for a house, this was where she would want it, the gentler winds and waters of False Bay notwithstanding.

She turned as he came out with the lunch, and she cleared a space on the table so that he could put the tray down. He had cut up mangoes and paw-paw, mixed them with fat Hanepoot grapes from the winelands beyond the Tygerberg range of mountains, and topped the lot with yoghurt. 'You're an artist with food as well as with paint,' she said when she'd spooned up a few mouthfuls. 'It tastes as good as it looks.'

He grinned. 'Thanks. We'll see if you enjoy future meals. Do you like curry?'

'Very much.'

'Good. It's one of my favourite dishes. A friend, a Malay fisherman, taught me how to make it. What's your speciality, Kirby?'

She thought for a moment. 'I've a fair hand with *sosaties*.'

'Now there's something I enjoy. We'll take turns at cooking shall we, Kirby? One night I'll make the meal, you'll do it the next.'

'Sounds like a nice idea,' she said, thinking how different he was from Jimmy, different indeed from all the other men she had known. She couldn't imagine any of them, willingly, spending time in a kitchen. Ross was able to do so without in any way diminishing his masculinity. In a way it seemed to make him even more of a man.

'I look forward to it.' He smiled, almost as if they were sealing a pact.

She found that despite any intentions to the contrary, she was looking forward to it too. After a moment she smiled back at him. It was hard not to respond to him. In a short time she had learned that much about the force of his personality.

'I thought you might have a housekeeper,' she said.

'I have Lena who comes in twice a week to do some house-cleaning. Other than that, I prefer the freedom of being on my own.'

'Then I would think that having me live with you here'—she stopped a moment, wondering whether to explain what she'd meant by the word 'live', then decided that would make her sound foolish—'would cramp your style.'

'On the contrary,' he said, with a look that brought a sudden flush to her cheeks. But before she could make anything of it, he said, 'Enjoy your lunch, Kirby.'

It would be hard not to enjoy it. The fruit was luscious. There were the sun and the sea and the mountains and the fresh salty air. And there was the attractive man—he *was* attractive, no matter how hard she might try to convince herself otherwise. A woman had only to look at him, to see his smile and to hear the vitality in his voice, to feel her senses responding with pleasure.

Was there any reason why she shouldn't enjoy herself? she asked herself. This was all so different from the hurried lunch-hour breaks she was accustomed to in the city. Okay, so she would be on her guard with Ross. She wouldn't let him sweet-talk her into bed—always supposing that was what he was after. A wry inner grin at the idea—as she'd already imagined him with all the world's most beautiful women, it seemed reasonable to suppose that he wouldn't be interested in her, Kirby. Which seemed to make it safe to relax and to have a good time.

He was leaning back in his chair, one leg crossed over the other. His legs were tanned and muscular, his feet, bare in thonged sandals, were big like his hands, with strong insteps and wide toes. A sailor or a fisherman, Kirby thought again.

'Been to any of the jazz festival concerts?' he asked.

'Two.' One with a free ticket passed on to her by Sally. The other with money she had saved through very frugal grocery-shopping.

'Which ones?'

'Jan Leroy and the Arthur Brothers.'

'I was at the Leroy concert. What did you think of him?'

'Excellent most of the time. But too contrived in the last number.'

Ross looked pleased. 'Almost the same words I used to Jan myself.'

Kirby was awed. 'You know Jan Leroy?'

'From way back. He stayed here a night before going back on the road.'

'Fantastic!' Kirby breathed, her image of cool sophistication slipping before her amazement. Jan Leroy was a legend in his own time. People slept all night in queues outside the booking-office to get tickets to his show—Sally had been heart-broken over having to miss it. And here was Ross Dolby, talking of him so casually, having actually had him as a guest in his home.

'Pablo didn't think it so fantastic.' Ross slanted a laughing look at the dog curled up in the shade. 'Jan's allergic to dogs, and poor Pablo had to spend the entire night locked up in the garage.'

'What would his fans say if they knew?' Kirby marvelled. 'Macho-men like Jan Leroy aren't supposed to be allergic to anything.'

'Don't tell his fans then.' Ross chuckled. 'Jan loves oysters, but not when they're live from the sea, and . . .'

He began to tell an anecdote that was both wicked and amusing. Fascinated, Kirby listened. Clearly Ross was not awed by the man he had entertained. His own stature was equal to that of Jan Leroy's, she realised, if not greater. He would know many famous people, he'd meet them on equal terms. What an interesting life he must lead, and how different his world must be from her own.

One anecdote led to another, more outrageous than the first, and Kirby laughed, the sound spontaneous and happy against the roar of the waves.

And then Ross said, 'The frown has vanished. And you have a lovely laugh, did you know that?'

For a while she'd been so absorbed in his stories that she'd forgotten about Kirby Lessard, single mother, career-minded and determined to remain detached from every man she met. The compliment brought her back to herself. Brought back the frown and the reserve that had been habitual for so long.

She was sure he would comment, and told herself she didn't care if he did. A few minutes ago she'd decided it was all right to relax. The compliment brought second thoughts. Ross was a man. And all men were the same basically. Weren't they?

But he did not comment. Perhaps he hadn't registered the frown after all, or the tightening of her body. 'What would you like to do this afternoon?' he asked.

'Doesn't that rather depend on you?'

'I'm going to be painting.'

'Oh, I see.' That left her at rather a loose end.

'Feel free to make yourself at home here in the house. And there's always the beach.' He gestured.

'I'm being paid to work.'

'We have worked.' The look he threw her was hard to read. 'Whether you want to admit it or not.'

She knew what he meant of course, because he'd explained it to her already. They'd talked, and they'd established a rapport of a sort. Not her idea of work, though it did seem to be his.

And somewhere inside her, was a perverse reaction at the thought that he had regarded their conversation as work and nothing more. I keep thinking I know myself, she reflected unhappily, and sometimes I find that I don't know myself as well as I thought.

A little brittlely, she said, 'But when will we start the real work?' She looked at him directly. 'You do know what I mean, Ross. I accept that you don't want me to use a note-book, but we have to have some sort of schedule.'

'I don't work to schedules. I thought by now you understood that.'

'I do . . .' She made a helpless gesture. 'But how will we do it?'

'As the whim takes us.' He laughed softly. 'I can't tell you when I'll feel like talking about myself. About My Life. That's how you think of it, isn't it? As if the words were capitalised?'

She sat stiffly, without answering him. In a way, that was how she did think of it. She'd been sent to do a job of work, and he was making it hard for her to do it. If he was laughing at her—and she had a suspicion that he was doing just that—he wasn't being very fair.

'Don't look so stricken,' Ross said. 'I will talk, I promise you. But it will have to be when the mood takes me.'

'Unfortunately you don't seem to know when that will be.'

'Does it matter? When I'm not painting we'll do things together. And when I feel like talking about myself, I will.' His eyes were on her face. 'You still look dubious. Don't you understand, Kirby? It will take time.'

'I hope my boss will understand.' Once more she felt the little frown between her eyebrows.

'He will if he wants the book. He'll understand that we have to get to know each other. That I can't just unburden myself to a stranger.'

'We'll always be strangers,' she said, the words coming out before she'd had time to think about them. In her own ears her voice sounded harsh.

'I don't think so,' Ross said. 'I really don't think so.'

*   *   *

In the end Kirby had a lovely afternoon. After lunch she helped Ross wash up—a matter of a minute—and then he vanished into his studio, and she went to the beach. She had her swimming-costume and a bottle of sun-tan oil. And to appease her conscience she brought a note-book and pen. There was little enough that she could say about Ross Dolby at this stage, but at least she could express her first impressions of the house, and of the man.

It was not all that hard to put down what she had seen of the house, but then she came to the man, and that was different. The Ross Dolby she was getting to know was an unusual man of extraordinary vibrance and magnetism. To try to describe him was difficult. Impossible. For half an hour Kirby played around with words, but Ross refused to rise from the page. The words were there, but they did not seem to do him justice.

So she put down the note-book and left it lying with the sun-tan oil while she walked to the edge of the water. It was one of those wonderful Cape days when the sky and the sea were blue and calm. There was just the hint of a breeze on a coastline where the wind was sometimes so strong that people could be blown down by its force.

She could never live willingly anywhere else but on the Cape Peninsula, Kirby often thought. Despite the fact that her flat was small and cramped and that she was determined to do better for herself and Meg, she loved Cape Town. There could be no city quite like it.

More than anything she loved the sea. Whenever she could she took Meg to the beaches on False Bay, to Muizenberg or Fish Hoek, where the water

was balmy and the little girl could play for hours
in the dying waves by the ocean's edge. So
different from this beach beneath Ross's house.

The smell of the salt and the sound of the waves
were exhilarating, but the water of the Atlantic on
this side of the Peninsula was just as icy as she'd
known it would be. She kept the toes of one foot
in the water just long enough to feel its numbing
effect, and then she began to walk along the sand,
enjoying the warmth of the sun on her face and
her body, the sand filtering through her toes;
stopping now and then to pick up a shell. Meg
loved shells, and Kirby looked for round smooth
ones to give her. Already she was missing her
child. Their first separation. Today was Monday,
she would not see the little girl till Saturday, or
perhaps Friday night. The one condition she had
made with Ross, weekends were her own.

It was going to be a long week.

It was to an Atlantic beach, much like this one,
that she had come on the day when she had found
out that Jimmy was not going to stand by her.
She'd been only nineteen at the time, and it had
seemed as if the world held no more hope for her.
All her dreams of a university education had been
shattered. Inside her a baby was growing. There
was no family who could help—Kirby had lost
both her parents during her teens—and the baby's
father had taken fright at the idea of the being
he'd helped create.

Perhaps if Kirby had pressed the issue Jimmy
might have given her some support, but even then,
in her youth and despair, she'd known it would be
futile. Jimmy was not ready for responsibility, and
a forced marriage—always supposing that she
would have been able to force it—would have been

disastrous. Kirby had been so sure that they loved each other. By the time that the pregnancy was confirmed she knew that they did not even like each other very much. There had only been a physical attraction between Jimmy and herself, a spark that had flared so brightly that one night she had lost control with no thought for the consequences.

She would not lose control again. She would not let herself get close to the point where she could fear losing control. It was a vow she had made on that beach, when she had known that her life had irrevocably changed.

She made the vow again now.

CHAPTER FOUR

Ross brought Kirby's suitcase into the house, and she unpacked while he got busy with the supper. An intriguing smell began to waft through to her from the kitchen. Curry, she guessed amused, as she went about putting her clothes in the lovely old Cape Dutch chest of drawers. Now and then she paused to stand at the open window and look out across the sea. It was beginning to get dark and the water had an opaque look about it, so that she could no longer distinguish the line that separated sea from sky. The air was fresh and salty, and the sound of the waves was a constant low thunder.

She turned and stood with her back to the window, and looked around her. She had switched on the lamp that stood on the bedside table, and it bathed the darkening room with a soft light. It was probably the loveliest room she had ever seen. Certainly the loveliest room she had ever slept in. Would she be sorry when the time came to leave it?

Her lips tightened at the thought. It was only a room for heaven's sake! A room was four walls with a ceiling. Some rooms were more appealing than others, but they were only rooms all the same. What mattered was the people inside them. And in Kirby's life there could be only one person. Meg. With movements that were suddenly angry she walked away from the window and went on unpacking.

She was putting her alarm-clock on the bedside-table when she saw the piece of paper on the bed. This time she knew right away what it was. Ross must have slipped the portrait into the room when he'd brought in the suitcase.

Her mouth softened as she picked it up. Freckles. No frown this time, but a face full of freckles. She peered in the mirror. Well, perhaps there were a few more freckles on her face than when she'd left for the beach. A mere handful more, and Ross didn't know her well enough to tell the difference. But he was an artist, and he painted what he felt or saw or was trying to convey, and she knew he was teasing her.

Mood lightening once more, she placed the portrait in her wallet with the first one. The weeks with Ross would be a time to remember. She'd never met anyone even remotely like him. Chances were she never would again. She could see herself telling Lynn about the strange man she was working with. Could see herself writing about him. Although he had not yet wanted to talk, already there were things she knew about him. Enough for her to perceive that Ross Dolby would capture the interest of others. He had certainly captured her own.

The curry was delicious, as she'd known it would be. Chunks of well-spiced meat eaten with rice and an exotic chutney. The afternoon on the beach had made Kirby hungry and she ate with zest.

'Did you swim?' Ross asked.

'If you call dipping the toes of one foot in the water swimming.' She laughed, her eyes sparkling in the soft light of amber candles. 'I'm not a martyr.'

'I'm glad to hear it.' Ross was smiling too, the smile which did such strange things to her nerve-stream despite her renewed vow to resist his appeal.

'I did some work.' She tried to suppress the sparkle as she steered the subject back to where it should rightfully be.

'With any success?'

'Not as much as I'd have liked. You've given me nothing to work with.'

'You're a single-minded woman. Have you always been this way, Kirby?'

She looked away from dark eyes that regarded her lazily yet intently. 'Not always.'

'How did you get so?'

Dangerous ground this. Ross Dolby would never know about the short-lived love-affair with Jimmy. About little Meg.

'I don't remember,' she said lightly. 'Besides, I'm the one who's supposed to be asking the questions.'

'As you remind me whenever possible.' If he had noticed the evasion he wasn't commenting on it.

'And you're still not willing to talk to me.' She helped herself to more curry. 'What about you, Ross? Did you have a good afternoon?'

'I did some sketching.'

'Including the freckled portrait.'

He smiled. 'That too.'

'I don't have that many freckles you know.'

'You will have after a few more days on the beach.' His chair was so close to hers that he was able to touch her face. She sat very still as he ran a finger along the bridge of her nose and drew light circles on her cheeks. 'Here,' he said, 'and here, this is where they'll be.'

His touch was doing the most appalling things to her senses. 'You don't know that,' she said a little jerkily. Really this was the most idiotic conversation.

'Does it matter?' There was an odd note in his voice. Almost as if he knew just what his touch was doing to her.

'No, of course not.' She hoped to put a quick end to this.

'I think it does.' His hand rested lightly on her cheek now. It did not move, it just lay there, and for some reason the sheer immobility was erotic.

'I'd like to see you with freckles and with your hair down,' Ross said. 'I'd like to paint you that way.'

'I can't imagine why.'

'Different image. More down to earth. A little primitive.'

'You talk absolute rubbish.' She pushed his hand abruptly away from her.

Mr Anderson would faint if he knew how she spoke to the famous and respected Ross Dolby.

'And it matters,' he said gently, 'because I'm being personal—and that gets you uptight every time.'

It was the very gentleness in his voice that brought her swinging round to look at him. Her eyes were big and green and a little troubled. 'Then why do you do it?'

'Because you intrigue me. Outwardly so cool and self-possessed. Except for the eyes, which you can't control. I want to know the real Kirby Lessard.'

'You'll be disappointed then, Ross. What you see is all there is.' She held out her glass. 'May I have some more wine, please?'

'You don't flatter yourself,' he said as he poured. 'Most of the women I've known have wanted me to think them mysterious—even if they weren't.'

'I must be different then.' Her smile hid the unspoken question—how many women had there been in his life?

'Yes, you're different.'

He sent her a look that swept from her face to her body, to linger for a moment on her breasts, before coming back to her face and her eyes once more. It was the kind of look which another man could have tried once only with Kirby—she had learned to deal with male looks. But she was unable to deal with this one, mainly because she did not know how to deal with the sudden desire that made nonsense of every resolution she had made.

It was with a sense of relief that she saw him push aside his plate. She had no idea how she was going to cope with a succession of candle-lit suppers if they were all going to be as disturbing as this one. For the moment she only wanted this one to end.

As before, they washed up together, a curiously intimate exercise in itself, and then Ross side-tracked her as she was about to go to her room. 'We'll go and sit a while in the library.'

'But I thought I'd . . .'

'It's early,' he said into the tiny pause that followed as she was thinking of an excuse. 'Please join me, Kirby.'

What could she do but give in to him? She followed him into a room that she had not seen before. As eclectic a room as her own, with a mixture of periods and styles that she was already beginning to find very appealing. Two walls were

book-lined, and a third had one of those huge
windows with a view, not over the sea but across
the slope of the mountain. On the remaining wall
was a small collection of masks. 'That one's from
Peru,' Ross said, following the direction of her
eyes. 'And the other two are west-coast Canadian.
Picked up on travels. Do you like them?' There
was something earthy about them which she liked
very much, and she told him so.

On an antique table near the window was a
copper sculpture. A young girl, her slender neck
drooping, her hands raised in a touching gesture of
appeal.

'She . . . seems alive,' Kirby said. 'Why is she so
sad?'

Ross did not answer. She did not know what
made her turn to look at him. He was looking at
her, and in his eyes was an expression which she
did not understand but which made her heart beat
suddenly faster. She wasn't sure how she suddenly
knew. 'You made this, didn't you?'

After a moment he said, 'Yes.'

'I didn't know you were also a sculptor.'

'I sculpt occasionally.'

Something had changed, and she didn't quite
know what, or why. She wondered if she'd
offended him in some way.

'She's beautiful,' Kirby said slowly. 'The kind of
piece you'd expect to see in a gallery.'

'She's never been for exhibition or sale.'

Ross's eyes were bleak. Kirby watched as he
went to the stereo and began to rummage through
a pile of records. There was something fierce in his
movements.

What did the sculpture mean to him? she
wondered. They'd both spoken of the work as

'she' never of 'it'. Of course it was an 'it', a piece
of copper, beautifully shaped and moulded. Yet it
was a 'she' too. A very real 'she' Kirby guessed.
Despite the fact that the piece had been sculpted
by an artist as brilliant as Ross Dolby, there was
something so poignant about the lovely copper
figure that she had to have been inspired by a real
person.

Someone who meant very much to Ross. Kirby
wished, very desperately, that the realisation did
not hurt her so much.

Ross must have found the record he wanted
because quite suddenly music flooded the room.
Trumpet music, loud and strident and a little
discordant to Kirby's ears. Ross said abruptly, 'Sit
down, Kirby, I'll get you a liqueur.'

She sat down in an armchair made of a soft
crumpled leather, and took the glass he brought
her. They did not talk, it would in fact have been
almost impossible to make conversation against
the music which Ross had turned so high that it
seemed to fill the room. Kirby sat quietly, sipping
her drink, her eyes going now and then to the
copper figure, and from there, when she was sure
that she was unobserved, to Ross. He'd looked so
tense when, after giving her the liqueur, he'd flung
himself down on a two-seater. But slowly the
tension seemed to have drained from him, so that
by the time the second side of the record was
almost at an end he appeared more relaxed. Kirby
had found the loud music a bit jarring. It seemed
to have had the opposite effect on Ross.

He put on another record, softer and more
mellow this time. Now and then he glanced at her,
and sometimes their eyes met, and Kirby was hard
put to hold his gaze. They did not talk, and she

was glad of the glass in her hand. She took tiny sips, hoping to make the drink last as long as she could, and she pretended to be concentrating on the music, but all the while she was not really listening at all. Ross looked relaxed now, but Kirby felt tense. As soon as she could she would make an excuse and retire to her room.

When the record ended she stood up. Ross looked at her enquiringly. 'You'd like to choose the next one?'

'Actually I'm off to bed.'

'Not yet. One more record, Kirby.'

'All right. But after that I really will say good night.'

He put on a piano concerto. 'Chopin?' she asked, recognising the music, not knowing whether she had the right piece.

'Chopin,' he confirmed.

'It's lovely.'

'One of my favourites,' Ross said.

He left the stereo, and went back to the two-seater. He sat down and leaned back, and gestured to the seat beside him. 'Come sit with me, Kirby.'

'No . . .' She gave him a tight smile.

He sat looking at her a moment, and then he got to his feet and came over to her. Before she could move he was sitting on the arm of her chair.

'Ross, I don't want . . .'

Her breath jerked as his arm went around her shoulder. 'Don't do that,' she said abruptly.

The arm remained where it was, and after a moment, Kirby said, 'Ross, please . . .'

She tried to move away from him, but his hand was holding her shoulder, she could feel the wool of his sweater against her cheek.

'Keep still,' he whispered.

'Take your arm away.'

He didn't move. She should be able to push his arm away, it wasn't as if he was holding her in a vice. But for a reason that she refused to analyse she seemed incapable of doing that.

'Ross, please . . .' she said again, a little desperately this time.

He bent his head and she felt his lips in her hair. 'Chopin was meant for touching.'

'No!'

'You can't listen to Chopin and not sit close to the person you're with.'

'You're just a crazy artist, you say things I've never heard anyone say before.'

'You might listen.'

'I can't . . .'

'Why? I'm not hurting you, Kirby. I'm just sitting close to you, feeling the warmth of your body, enjoying the music. Why don't you do the same?'

'I don't go in for touching,' she said in a hard flat voice.

'Everyone needs to be touched.' His voice was so quiet, so tender. If he was sweet-talking her he was doing it in a way no man had done with her before. She felt unsettled, disturbed. And stirring inside her was an ancient longing. She'd felt something like it once before, with another man, but it had been nothing like this. She didn't want to feel it, she would give anything to push it away. But it was a basic, primitive feeling, and she didn't know how to rid herself of it.

For at least two minutes they sat quite still, Ross with his arm around Kirby's shoulder. The lovely harmonies of the piano concerto filled the room, but Kirby hardly heard them. Her ears were filled with the sound of Ross's heart-beats. She heard them, she could feel them against her cheek, right through his sweater. She could smell the clean male smell of him, it seemed to fill her nostrils.

'Not so bad, is it?' he asked at length.

Such a casual phrase to describe the whole tumultuous orbit of her feelings.

'I won't go to bed with you.'

'We're nowhere near that yet.'

'It's not a question of yet,' she said fiercely. 'It's ever.'

'Men and women were meant to go to bed together, Kirby.'

'Not this woman! Understand that, Ross. We'll be working together, nothing more.'

He took so long to answer that she thought she'd got through to him at last. And then he turned her to him, folding her against his chest with the arm that still held her shoulders. With the other hand he cupped her face—such a big hand, her face fitted snugly into its palm—and tilted her head so that she had to look at him.

The awful thing was that she was letting him get away with it. Dimly she remembered the vow she had made on the beach that afternoon, knew that she had to get away from him. But her brain seemed quite unable to send the correct messages to her body. Perhaps because the sensations flooding her body drowned out any messages it received.

He bent his head, and even then she was unable to move. His lips came down on hers. It was a light kiss, tender and experimental, giving sweetness and demanding nothing in return. Something primeval, deep inside Kirby, seemed to beg her to open her lips, to return the kiss, but she didn't. Sanity enough remained to let her keep her lips tightly closed.

He lifted his head at last. 'I believe you can do better than that.'

'I don't know what you mean,' she said coldly.

But she did know. Oh, she knew.

'How old are you, Kirby?'

Here it came. The mockery, the contempt. She'd been through all of it before with other men. And had dealt with it very satisfactorily.

'Twenty-two.'

'And so untouched.' There was a kind of wonder in his voice.

Most men ridiculed her for her prudery. She had expected Ross to do the same, but Ross, she was learning, was not one to do what others did.

And his power was all the more lethal for it.

'Yet not quite untouched, surely?' he asked. 'At twenty-two. And so pretty.'

'Not quite,' she conceded. 'Ross, I meant what I said about not going to bed with you.'

His expression changed suddenly, she saw the lifting of his lips at the corners, the sparkle in his eyes. 'You could try it.'

'You're crazy! Didn't you understand what I said?'

'I heard. I'm not sure I understood.'

He bent his head again, and this time there was a hint of passion in his kiss, and it was even harder than before for Kirby to keep from responding.

When he lifted his head again there was a speculative look in his eyes. 'I'm not convinced.'

'You should be. This isn't what I want, Ross.' Her throat was raw and dry.

'How can you know till you've tried it?'

'You speak as if sex is fun.'

'It is fun, Kirby.'

And she had thought him different from other men—she must have been mad. Fun was what it had been for Jimmy, until the shock of hearing the consequences of his fun. Fun was all it was for Ross.

'It might be a good idea for you to go to bed with me.'

'I don't think so.'

'It would make for rapport between us.'

'We don't need that kind of rapport.'

'Think what it could do for the book.'

So Ross had his own techniques—foolish of her to have thought otherwise, even for a moment. Well, he would have to see where they got him. Pleasantly she observed, 'We'll still get the book done.'

It took an effort of will, but she managed to lever herself away from him and out of the chair. And this time Ross did not persuade her to stay.

'Good night.' Her voice as firm as she could make it.

'Good night, Kirby,' she heard him say, very softly, as she went from the room.

Hours later Kirby was still awake. She lay in bed, listening to the thundering of the surf and the howling of the wind that had risen in the last hours. As a Capetonian she was used to wind, but the apartment she shared with Meg was in a relatively sheltered position. Ross's house on the cliff was far more vulnerable. It was like being on a ship, she thought. You could almost feel the buffeting of the elements. Depending on the kind of person you were, you'd find it either nerve-wracking or thrilling. It would be the latter emotion for Ross. His surprising gentleness notwithstanding, she sensed in him a pagan wildness that would find kinship with the wind.

It was a wind that suited Kirby's mood tonight. She didn't know how long she'd been lying awake, her mind in turmoil as she relived the day, the last hour in particular.

What was happening to her? She'd been so certain that she was finally in control of her emotions and her life. Until today there had been no problems.

She'd sensed on Friday that Ross Dolby could mean danger. But even then she hadn't conceived the extent of it. If she had, she would have refused the assignment, no matter the consequences. Her career was important to her, but remaining free of emotional involvement was even more important. Yet she had let herself be persuaded by her boss— and at this stage it might be impossible to withdraw without losing all future respect and credibility.

Somehow she would have to find a way of living with Ross in this house on the wild Atlantic cliff. But how? This afternoon on the beach she had made a promise to herself. She'd thought then that she'd have little trouble keeping it.

Now she no longer knew what to think.

For what was keeping her awake tonight was not so much Ross as herself. His advances had been no more persistent than those of other men, less so perhaps. He hadn't forced himself on her, in fact it was his gentleness that had surprised her. For there was passion in the man. She could sense it, contained, held in check, but very much in existence all the same.

She was quite alone with him in this house, with nobody for miles on either side. But that was not what frightened her. Ross Dolby was not a violent man. He would not force himself on her, would not hurt her in any way. What frightened Kirby was herself. If she had had nobody to rely on, she had always known she could rely on herself. For the first time it occurred to her that she might be deluding herself. Her body had betrayed her tonight. Her emotions. There had been sensations she had been unable to suppress. A longing that was so primitive that it had shaken her with its strength.

She still felt as shaken now as she had been then. Sex, love, these things were not for her. She'd done with them. Meg and her career were the only things in her life that mattered—how often had she told herself that. Give in to the demands of sex, and she would lose her precious independence.

She got out of bed and opened the window. The wind hurled the surf so high that the spray reached the house. Leaning out of the window she took long breaths of air that was as sparkling as champagne. Tonight she had been caught off her guard. She would take care that it did not happen again.

She was up early the next morning. After she'd showered and dressed she left her room and walked through the house to the patio. Of Ross there was no sign. She went to the very edge of the patio and sniffed the salt of a sea that had calmed somewhat since the previous night. What Ross did for breakfast she had no way of knowing, but she was hungry. Good, she thought, she would be able to eat alone.

Going back to the kitchen, she put a slice of bread in the toaster and plugged in the electric kettle. As she waited for the water to boil she looked curiously around her. The kitchen was modern, with all the conveniences a person could want, and yet even here Ross had imprinted his personality. On the wall were copper pots that might have belonged in an old-style farmhouse kitchen, and yet far from looking out of place amidst the wood surfaces and the chrome, they were just right in the room. Above the sink was a frieze of tiles, each with a picture of a different herb, delicately and rather picturesquely executed. Near the window stood a small round oak table, on it an earthen jar filled with wild grasses. It was the kind of kitchen in which a woman would enjoy cooking, where she'd want to try out new and exotic dishes. For a moment Kirby could see herself cooking here—only for a moment though, for then she pushed the picture from her mind.

She took her tea and toast to the oak table, and sat where she could see through the window on to the mountain. The slope against which the house was built was rugged, with lots of bare rock and some scrub, and a few trees that were bent from the wind. Here and there near the house were patches of colour where proteas grew wild. High over a *krans* an eagle hovered, and through the scrub scampered a *dassie*. Kirby watched the little rock-rabbit, and for a few moments she was smiling.

It was going to be another gorgeous day, perfect for sunbathing. But that was not her purpose for being here. Which brought her thoughts to Mr Anderson.

When she'd rinsed her plate and cup she went to

the 'phone. Her boss was a workaholic who arrived at the office at sunrise. He would be there now.

'Why, Kirby.' He sounded surprised to hear her voice. 'Run into a problem?'

It was only right that he should know how things stood. She took a breath. 'I'm not doing any work.'

'You've only been there a day.'

'I know. But we could have done something. Ross ... Mr Dolby could have started dictating. Do you know what I did yesterday, Mr Anderson? I helped him fix a fishing-net.'

Her boss chuckled. 'Did you have fun?'

Kirby's fingers tightened on the receiver. Mr Anderson was sounding like Ross.

Carefully she said, 'I don't know if today will be any different.'

'Has he said he won't dictate?'

'No, but he hasn't said that he will. He says he will talk when the mood takes him, Mr Anderson, and I have no idea when that will be. And no note-book and pencil, any notes I make are to be in my head.'

'The best place for them to be sometimes,' said her boss unexpectedly. 'All right, Kirby, I know what you're getting at. Ross Dolby is not what you expected.'

'I've never met anyone like him.'

'Perhaps that's what makes his work so exceptional. He's a great man, Kirby. Stay where you are and be patient, and don't worry if you're not earning your bread every day. You'll get your story eventually, and when you do it will be worth it.'

And with that she had to be content. She'd

understood last night that she couldn't ask to be relieved of the assignment. But she'd hoped that Mr Anderson would do the relieving of his own accord, that he'd send someone else here to Ross, and give Kirby a chance to ghost-write another biography. Apparently that was not to be. Remembering how strangely Mr Anderson had behaved on Friday, when she'd gone to see him after seeing Ross, she realised that she should not be surprised.

She phoned Lynn next. 'Meg's fine,' said her friend. 'Missing you, but fine. Here, darling, say hello to Mommy.'

Kirby closed her eyes as the tiny voice came to her through the line. It was the first time she and Meg had been apart. She wanted to see her, hug her, hold her in her arms. And she reminded herself that she was putting herself through this ordeal—for it would be an ordeal—for Meg's sake. In order for Meg to have all the things Kirby wanted for the child, she had to make a success of her career.

Lynn came to the 'phone. 'Are you getting on with Mr Dolby?'

'He's not the easiest man to get on with,' Kirby said shortly.

'Oh dear.' There was a note of mischief in Lynn's voice.

'I'll see you on Saturday,' Kirby said. 'I hate this separation.'

'I know you do.'

'It's going to be a long week.'

'I've a feeling I'd enjoy it. Don't worry about Meg.'

'I'll be counting the days till Saturday,' Kirby said, and then she said goodbye.

She was putting down the receiver when

something made her turn. Ross stood in the doorway, an odd look in his eyes.

'I didn't hear you come in.' Kirby felt suddenly flustered.

He shrugged, and then his mouth lifted slightly. 'Good morning,' he said.

CHAPTER FIVE

'GOOD morning.' Her voice was slightly breath-less—did he hear it?—but she managed to treat him to a cool smile.

'Sleep well?'

'Yes, thank you.' She gestured. 'I hope you didn't mind me using the 'phone.'

'Of course not, feel free. Any more calls to make?'

'No.'

How much had he heard? How long had he been in the room? Well, she was certainly not going to ask him.

'You must be hungry,' he said.

'I've eaten. I didn't see you around. I thought it would be all right.'

'Of course.' For the first time he smiled. 'I want you to feel at home.'

Which was a very different thing from *being* at home. I'm ridiculous, Kirby thought. Aloud she said, 'What are we going to do today?'

'The very question I was going to ask you. Do you have any plans, Kirby?'

He was dressed as before in shabby jeans and a faded T-shirt which clung snugly to the broad chest so that she could see the suggestion of muscles beneath the fabric. His throat and arms, tanned and strong, were bare. His face had a wind-stung freshness as if he had just spent an hour walking along the beach. Pity he hadn't knocked on her door and woken her, she'd have loved to have walked with him in the salty morning air.

'My plans seem to depend on you.' She wished her words did not sound quite so prim. 'Aren't we going to do some work, Ross?'

'I'd hoped your conscience would have stopped jabbing you by now.' He was laughing at her, his eyes warm with the sparkle that brought out the golden depths lurking in the brown. 'I'm going to paint this morning, Kirby.'

'Oh . . .'

'I'll be in the studio most of the morning. So your plans really depend on you.'

Ross would start talking about his life when the mood took him, he'd said. And Mr Anderson didn't mind. So why should she? It was time indeed for her conscience to stop its jabbing. Besides, she had the feeling that Ross would respect her more if she showed that she was her own woman. Which was what she was anyway.

She smiled suddenly, without the cool reserve this time. 'Fine. I'll just do my own thing too in that case.'

Which meant going to the beach, she decided, when Ross had vanished in the direction of the studio. She went to her room, and changed into her sedate one-piece swimsuit, sorry that she'd left her bikini at home, for the bikini flattered her in a way that this costume did not. But figure-flattery was not what she was after while she stayed alone with Ross Dolby. Not after last night, she thought, and felt her cheeks warm. Especially not after last night.

She pulled pants and a blouse over the swimming-costume and then she saw that the chignon he hated had come loose. She was standing at the mirror, a handful of pins held between her lips, about to push her hair back into

place, when she let the pins drop. Ross did not
care what she did, and neither, it seemed, did Mr
Anderson. So few holidays came her way, she
might as well enjoy what seemed to be turning into
one while she could.

Yesterday she'd asked Ross if she could borrow
books from his library, and he'd said yes. There
were beautiful art books that she wanted to see,
but she could not risk sand getting into the pages.
She felt differently about a worn-looking paperback, Ross would not mind her taking it to the
beach, she felt sure. Her knowledge of art was not
great, and this book might give her some of the
background she needed.

Whistling to Pablo, she took the steep path that
led down to the beach. The water was that deep
indigo blue which she loved, and the sand was
unmarked by human feet since the last tide. Only
the tiny tendril marks of gulls marred the
smoothness, and then Pablo, hurtling joyfully
across the beach, left a haphazard trail of his own.

Kirby spread her towel on the sand, oiled her
body and lay down, pillowing her head on her
beach-bag. Having decided to let her conscience
rest, she realised that this was bliss. Four hours
stretched before her. Well no, perhaps three, for
though Ross would probably work until one,
Kirby meant to be dressed and in the kitchen with
the *sosaties* on the stove long before he came out
of the studio.

For a while she read. No wonder the book had
been paged through so often. It was a gem of
information, and Kirby was soon absorbed.
Having realised some time ago that the education
which was so important to her, and which had
been denied her by the birth of her darling Meg,

was available in a different way, she had become a voracious reader. This book covered art forms of many different periods. Since she was going to be writing about an artist, the more she knew about art the better.

For at least an hour she read, while Pablo raced this way and that, sniffing at the waves and trying in vain to catch seagulls, and then the sun and the heat got the better of Kirby, and she put down the book and closed her eyes.

She wasn't sure what woke her. Her eyes opened and there was Ross standing not two feet away from her. He looked very tall, very rugged and strong as he towered above her, and she felt something stir inside her that she did not want to feel.

She sat up, and wished she had a way of covering herself. She'd been going to beaches all her life, for heaven's sake, she practically *lived* on the beach at weekends, she and Meg, and being in a swimming-costume had never bothered her before. And yet at this moment she felt uncertain and vulnerable. Which might have something to do with the expression on Ross's face. Not a leer, that she could deal with. But an enigmatic expression which she could not define. Which she did *not want* to define, she decided after a moment.

'I must have fallen asleep,' she said, a little jerkily.

'Nothing wrong with that.' He was smiling. 'Except for the doubtful wisdom of getting burnt when you're not conscious of it.'

I'm in danger of being burned by something stronger than the sun, she thought.

Ross squatted down beside her. 'You let your hair down,' he said softly.

She'd forgotten all about her hair! Her hands went to it in a swift movement. She felt colour flood her face, and cursed herself for the reaction that she was unable to prevent.

'What time is it?' she asked.

'Elevenish.'

She thought she couldn't have slept all that long. She'd reckoned herself safe from Ross's eyes for much longer.

'You should be working, shouldn't you?' The question sounded a little like an accusation. 'Didn't you say you'd be in the studio all morning?'

'A man can change his mind.' He looked amused. Also intrigued. As if he had registered her defensiveness, and understood the reason for it.

Kirby bit her lip. She couldn't reproach him for not keeping to his painting hours. He'd think she was crazy, and besides, to all intents and purposes, what he did had nothing to do with her. Except that by cutting short his work he had caused her extreme confusion. Which was one more thing she could not tell him.

'I like your hair this way,' he said.

He was wearing shorts, and his bare thighs were very close to her. She saw the tautness of the bent legs, the hair that curled on the tanned skin. The strong muscles. What would it be like to dance with him? Or to lie in bed with him?

I don't believe I asked myself that, she thought horrified, a moment later. She felt a little dizzy. She wanted very much to put her hair up again, but the fact that she had left the pins in the room was not the only reason she could not do so. Ross had already guessed that she felt stripped before him, that she needed some kind of armour—

having the knowledge confirmed would give him a power over her that she did not want him to have.

'Why don't you wear it like this always?' he asked.

'I like it up.' She searched for a topic that would divert his attention. 'Pablo has been having a fantastic time. I don't think you take him out enough.'

Ross laughed. 'Nobody could have enough energy for Pablo.' His gaze rested affectionately on the dog, then returned to Kirby. 'Do you wear your hair up on weekends?'

'Why this interest in my hair?' she asked, nervousness edging her voice with impatience.

'Because it's beautiful—the thickness, and the different shades of honey and gold.' He paused. When he went on his voice had changed. 'There's another reason. I can't help wondering about the Kirby you show to other people.'

She stared at him, not sure what he was getting at. And then he said, 'You seem very keen to go home on weekends.'

Had he found out about Meg? She stiffened, immediately on her guard. She would have no snide comments about her daughter or her way of life. She did not tolerate them from other men, she did not have to take them from Ross Dolby, famous artist notwithstanding.

'I am keen,' she acknowledged flatly.

The eyes that lingered on her face were intent. 'Is there a man, Kirby?'

Suddenly she understood. 'You were listening to my conversation.'

'Unintentionally. I came into the room and didn't realise you were there. You've a quiet voice . . . I heard the tail-end of the conversation.'

'You could have walked out,' she pointed out.

'I could have,' he acknowledged. 'I didn't.'

She'd wondered when he'd come into the room how much he had heard. At the time she'd felt a little put out. Now she realised that she could put what he had picked up—and misunderstood—to good advantage.

'Yes, there's a man,' she said, without a qualm at the lie.

She was in danger every moment that she remained in Ross Dolby's company. She could lose her peace of mind, her precious independence of spirit. If last night had taught her anything, it was that emotions and sensations she had thought dead were not dead at all. She had learned too that her emotions were not always hers to control.

She did *not want* to feel. She did *not want* to think of herself as sexual or passionate, as a person with feelings. Feelings made you vulnerable, and she never wanted to feel vulnerable again. Yet even now she was feeling. Just the closeness of Ross's strong body was enough to make her feel. If he knew just how strongly she felt he would press his advantage and make love to her. Ross was a man, wasn't he? And all men took their fun where they could get it.

So she'd let him think there was a man in her life. It would explain a lot. Even if it was the wrong explanation.

'Someone important?' he asked.

Why on earth was he so interested? 'A good friend.'

'The comment people give when they're being interviewed by the press.' He laughed quietly, but his eyes were strangely unamused. 'I wouldn't like the woman who meant something to me to refer to me as a good friend.'

Did that mean there was such a woman? Short of asking—which she would not do—Kirby had no way of knowing. And she wished that knowing did not matter so much to her.

He stretched down beside her on the sand, just inches from her towel, his hands clamped behind his head. Closing his eyes, he let the sun warm his face, as Kirby had done earlier. It was safe to look at him. At the rugged face, at the tanned skin and high cheek-bones. At the thick eye-lashes, and the shadows they cast. At the lips, moulded and firm, and yet sensuous at the same time. Lips that had been on hers less than twenty-four hours ago.

With an effort Kirby tore her eyes from Ross. There had been something almost hungry in the way she had looked at him, as if she needed to commit every detail of his face to memory. And that was ridiculous, obscene. Against everything she had decided, against everything she believed in. It was not as if she was in love with the man. Love was for the naïve, for those who could let themselves put all their trust in a man, ignorant of the fact that one day the trust would be betrayed. Love was not for her.

Which still did not explain why Ross affected her as strongly as he did.

It had to be physical. A peculiar chemistry. All the things one read about and which she did not want to believe. At least not of herself. Okay, she acknowledged that a person had physical needs, Meg was proof of that. But it was desperately important for her to know that they were needs that could be suppressed, controlled. She could control them, of course. No way was she going to give in to the quite absurd urge to stretch out a hand and touch the strand of dark hair that had

fallen over Ross's forehead. But what she wished
was that she could suppress the *need* to do so.

'Why aren't you married to him?' Ross asked.

His eyes were still closed, she saw that in the
brief glance she allowed herself. Nevertheless she
made herself look away from him again and back
at the sea.

'No particular reason.'

'Are you going to marry him?'

'Perhaps.'

'Seems an iffy kind of relationship.'

'It's not iffy at all.'

'And it's none of my business,' he suggested
lazily.

'Right,' she agreed firmly. 'It isn't. I couldn't
care less about the women in your life, I wouldn't
dream of asking you why you're not married.'

'I'd tell you if you did.'

It was not the answer she expected. She was
suddenly rigid. I don't care enough to ask, were
the words that hovered on her tongue. But the
question she asked aloud was, 'Why aren't you?'

His eyes opened. She was unprepared for the
hand that caught her wrist, for the fingers that
caressed the soft inner skin just above it. 'I've
never felt I wanted to.'

If only it wasn't such an effort to stay relaxed. 'I
wouldn't believe it if you said there'd been no
women in your life,' she said stiffly.

His laugh was low and came from his throat.
'There've been many women, Kirby, you know
that. Just nobody that I cared enough about to
marry.'

'So you'll end your life as a bachelor.'

'I didn't say that.'

What was he saying then? She wished that it did

not matter to her what he did, what he thought, and how he chose to live his life and with whom. She wished that she didn't feel so utterly wretched and confused.

'Time to start on the *sosaties*,' she said, and made to stand up. Only to find that the hold on her wrist was stronger than she'd realised.

'Don't run away,' he said softly.

'I'm not running.'

'We can have *sosaties* another day. Does he mind, Kirby?'

'Mind?' she asked a little stupidly.

'Your man. Does he mind that you're going to be living with me?'

The stroking movement above her wrist had become more sensuous, and her heart was beating just a little too fast.

'He knows I won't be living *with* you. Not in the sense that you're implying.'

'He can't be sure of that.' Ross's tone was lazy, and all the more outrageous for it. 'How can he be, when you're not sure yourself?'

The breath caught in her throat. 'I'm sure,' she said then.

'Are you?' It was asked very quietly.

She swung round to look at him. His eyes were on her and there was nothing lazy in the glance that lingered on her lips, and then on her throat and the swell of her breasts.

'Quite sure,' she said tightly. 'If you heard me talking to him, you also heard me saying I couldn't wait for the weekend.'

'I heard.' He was smiling, but it was hard to read his eyes.

'Then we all know where we stand.'

'We don't know a thing, and if you think

otherwise you're a fool.' His voice was suddenly hard. '*Do* you wear your hair down on weekends?'

'That's none of your business either.'

'I'm curious all the same.'

The hand on her wrist jerked suddenly, so that she was caught off balance and fell against him. His other hand went beneath her hair, cupping the back of her head. He was so close to her that she could feel every inch of the long sun-warmed body against her own. Her heart, which had been beating fast since the conversation began, now pounded so loudly that she thought he must hear it above the sound of the waves.

'You intrigue me.' His lips were like a brand of fire against her throat. 'That's why I'm curious.'

'Ross . . .'

'Yes, Kirby, I'll kiss you.'

She tasted the salt on his lips as her own lips parted beneath them. And his body was hard where it pressed against hers. Trembling with a desire that sprang to life with all the suddenness of a veld-fire, Kirby lifted her hands to his head, her fingers threading through his hair, pulling him closer toward her. He would never be close enough, never.

Sanity returned suddenly, and she pushed him away from her, pushed him violently and a little too hard, because he responded immediately, so that she realised that perhaps she'd only had to ask.

They faced each other on the sand, Kirby was trembling and Ross looked strangely tense.

After a moment he said, 'You see, your man can't know where he stands, because we don't know ourselves.'

*   *   *

That afternoon he took her fishing. She protested at first, after the morning she'd spent she was in no mood to be in his company. But her protest was over-ridden. Ross wanted her to go fishing with him, and when Ross had made up his mind about something he was a hard man to argue with.

Just say one word about what happened on the beach this morning, and I'll go straight back to the house, she warned silently.

But Ross said nothing. He whistled while they walked along the wet sand, the fishing-rods slung across one shoulder, a canvas bag that had seen better days and which presumably contained bait and other fishing paraphernalia, hanging from the other. Now and then he threw an old tennis-ball to Pablo.

He was behaving as if nothing was further from his mind than the kisses they'd exchanged just a few hours earlier. He'd probably forgotten the incident almost as soon as it happened. Well, not forgotten exactly, for his memory wouldn't be that bad, but he'd ceased to give it any thought. A couple of casual kisses was all there had been. Nothing much to Ross, who'd had so many women in his life. He'd told her about the women himself.

If only the kisses had meant as little to Kirby. As she relived them now—unwillingly—her cheeks flamed with angry colour. Just as well they meant nothing to Ross. It would make it easier for her to forget them herself.

And she wished she believed that.

At a great pile of craggy rock they stopped. 'This is where we're going to fish?' Kirby asked, and Ross nodded. Little pools of foamy water eddied around the bottom of the rock-pile, creamy and sun-warmed and waiting for the next tide to carry them out. Shells clung everywhere, so that in places you couldn't see even a square inch of rock-face. They were dark and wet and prickly underfoot. Pablo was still sniffing them, trying in vain to pry them loose as the two humans began to climb.

'Need some help?' Ross asked once, turning back as he went. Kirby shook her head. She'd been climbing rocks all her life, and besides, she didn't want his help. Just near the top though they came to a chasm that was wider than the rest, and Kirby debated whether to jump across—and risk a fall on the slippery shells—or whether to do the undignified thing and make her way sitting/sliding over the rock-face. Ross turned at that moment. Without a word he reached down a hand to her. Kirby hesitated only a moment before taking it. It was a strong hand, cool and firm on hers, pulling her easily across the chasm.

They reached the top, and Ross put down the rods and opened the bag. Kirby watched as he busied himself with the hooks and bait. He seemed so at home here, on these rocks, in a pair of disreputable jeans rolled up to the knees, and a stained figure-hugging sweater.

'I'd like to take a photo of you like this,' she said.

He looked up at her. 'You would?'

'For the book.' It seemed necessary to say it, though it should have been obvious. But she didn't want him to think it was for herself. He would never know if she kept an extra copy as a memory.

'Well, another time, when you've a camera with you,' he said. 'We're ready to go, Kirby. Ever fished?'

Strangely, she hadn't. No use telling him otherwise, he would see in an instant that she was a novice. 'I've watched often enough,' she told him.

'Here then.' He gave her a rod. 'Have a try.'

From the vantage-point of the sand it always looked so easy when the fishermen cast their lines out to sea. With the rod actually in her hand—and heavier than she'd expected it to be—the operation was much more difficult. Kirby swung it back and let the line out, and watched as it drooped miserably at the bottom of the rocks.

'Let me show you,' Ross offered.

Hastily she said, 'I'm sure I can manage,' and threw the rod again.

'Better, but not good enough.' Ross came up beside her. 'I'm going to teach you the right way to do it.'

'I don't think it's necessary,' she protested jerkily.

'For the girl who's going to ghost-write my life it is.' He was grinning at her.

She didn't want him teaching her, not if it meant that he was going to be touching her, and she had a feeling he would be doing just that. 'I'm going to be writing about an artist,' she said.

'And a fisherman.' He was looking down at her, and his eyes were sparkling. 'Ready, Kirby?'

Short of making a fool of herself, there was really nothing she could do to stop him. She had to let him stand behind her, his arms enfolding her, his hands over hers on the rod.

'Just concentrate on getting the movement right.' He was so close to her that she could feel his breath in her ear and it took no effort at all to hear his voice above the sound of the waves. 'Don't worry for the moment where the line falls.'

Kirby was only conscious of the body so close to hers that she could feel its whipcord strength all the length of her back. Her shoulders seemed to fit into the curves of his armpits, and his legs were taut against hers. His hands were wide and strong, huge tanned hands lying on small soft ones that trembled a little beneth his grip. The wretched fishing-line was the very least of her worries.

'Like this,' he said. 'Feel the movement, Kirby.'

It was the most erotic movement she had ever experienced. As he swung the rod back over their shoulders, he swung Kirby with it, his body, his hands, never breaking contact with hers. His arms were against hers, tight and hard, her face was against his chest, the smell of the man mingled with the salty smell of the sea, and her legs and back were arched and strained across his legs and chest. For a timeless moment they were two bodies merged into one, straining together in one fluid motion. Two bodies in identical pose, with the wind and spray stinging their faces, and their arms flung high as if in some kind of victory.

And then he was moving her again, forward this time, with the same fluid speed. Now their arms were pointing downwards, toward the water, and it was his body that lay against hers.

'That's it,' he cried, and she wasn't sure if she actually heard the words or if she just felt them against her neck.

'See the line, Kirby?'

The stupid line again. The fact that it had hit the water a fair distance from the rocks, that was what meant something to Ross. He was just a fisherman teaching a woman how to cast a line—any woman—and the erotic closeness of their bodies had not moved him in the least. Chances were, in the concentration of the moment he had not even noticed it. To Ross the fishing-line was everything. To Kirby it was meaningless. What mattered was the man, and the feel of his body, and the sensations he had stirred up inside her.

So much for good intentions.

'Again,' he said.

Impossible to go through with it again. The whole thing hadn't lasted more than a minute, but it had left Kirby felling dizzy and confused, and aching with a desire which appalled her even while she recognised it for what it was. His arms were still around her, his hands over hers on the rod, his legs braced tautly behind her, holding them both so that they would not slide into the ocean.

'No!' she shouted.

Either Ross didn't hear the protest or otherwise he chose to ignore it. He drew in the line, and then once more the rod was cast back, and then forward. Again the two bodies moved in unison. Once more the world spun before Kirby's eyes.

'I think I've got it now.'

He didn't respond, and she turned to repeat the words. And was disconcerted to find that her mouth was on a level with his shoulders, and that she had to tilt her head to make herself heard.

'Good.' He was still holding her, and she saw his gaze go from her eyes to her lips.

He was going to kiss her. Her breath caught in her throat, so that she couldn't tell him not to. Twisted against him, with his arms still around her, she couldn't even move.

But he didn't kiss her. Quite gently, he took his hands from hers, and took a step away from her, and she had to steady herself to keep from falling.

'Let's see you try then,' he said in a neutral voice.

'It might not be perfect. It'll take some practice.'
Her voice matched his for casualness.

But inside her, as she readied herself to cast the
rod, there was a kind of turmoil. She'd wanted
him to kiss her. She'd known it the moment he had
let her go. And the depths of her wanting terrified
her.

CHAPTER SIX

KIRBY caught no fish, but Ross hauled in two, and with that he was satisfied. 'Just right for our supper,' he said.

They packed away the fishing-tackle and made their way back down the rocks. They'd eat on the beach, Ross said, and they began to gather driftwood for a fire while Pablo raced around as energetically as before.

The sun was beginning to set by the time the first flames crackled from the wood. Kirby sat close to it, drawing up her legs so that she could rest her chin on her knees, watching as Ross cleaned the fish as expertly as she'd known he would. Now and then the fire needed fresh wood. The first time Ross threw some on the flames, then Kirby took over.

The darkening sky was rather beautiful, she thought, not ablaze but awash with twilight colours. 'Do you find this inspirational?' she asked, and Ross looked up at her and smiled without answering, then returned his attention to the fish.

As Kirby watched the large competent hands, she was aware of something stirring inside her. Some of the desire she'd felt on the rocks still lingered. It was the strangest feeling, unsettling and disturbing, so that she was restless and a little on edge. She didn't want him to make love to her—and at the same time she wanted it desperately.

91

Firmly she shifted her eyes and looked in the direction of Cape Town. Less than an hour's drive from here, and yet it could have been at the other end of the world. She put her mind to picturing Meg. Lynn would be feeding her now, and then the little girl would play for a while with her toys before Lynn put her to bed. Every detail of the scene was summoned to mind. Meg in her pale pink pyjamas, with the baby-soft fair hair falling over her forehead, her cheeks a little flushed after her bath. Meg's cot, with the Disney pictures pasted on the head and footboards, and the shabby but beloved teddy, which had once belonged to Kirby, lying in one corner. Lynn's spare bedroom, Meg's home until her mother's assignment was finished.

I miss my baby. Oh, I miss her so much, Kirby thought resentfully. But for Ross Dolby's insistence that she stay even at night in his isolated home, she would be with her daughter now.

It was terrible, but Meg seemed almost as far as the city. At this moment the reality was the beach and the fire and the crazy dog. And the crazier man, who claimed he was an artist, and looked and behaved anything but.

Reality was also the deepening feeling that moved inside Kirby every time she looked at him.

'I've only your word for it that you're really Ross Dolby,' she mused.

He looked up at her with a grin. 'It's the name my parents gave me when I was born.'

'I believe you're an impostor.' It was easier to tease at this moment than to be formal with him. 'You're not at all like an artist.'

'You've known so many in your time?' The question was seriously put, but she knew he was teasing too.

'A girl is allowed an imagination. You flout every concept I ever had about emaciated artists living on inspiration and cheese and wine.'

'Which disappoints you.'

It didn't disappoint her at all. He was so very attractive, this large, tanned man with the rugged face, and the dark eyes with that far-seeing look as if he'd spent his life scanning distant horizons.

'Naturally,' she said.

His grin had deepened, as if her teasing delighted him. And after a moment she grinned back at him. She could not have resisted.

Before long the fish were grilling. By the time they were ready it was already quite dark. Ross threw some more wood on the fire which had become a little island of light on the lonely beach.

'Delicious,' Kirby pronounced when she'd had her first mouthful of fish flavoured with lemon and smelling of smoke.

'Had to be good. Caught and cooked by an expert.' There was laughter in his voice.

For a moment he was quiet, and then he said, 'I started life as a fisherman. You were right about that, Kirby.'

Something in his tone made her look up quickly. In the dim light of the fire she saw that the laughter had vanished from his face. He seemed almost to be looking inwards at himself. She was about to respond to his remark, but some instinct kept her silent.

'The ocean is a part of me,' Ross went on at last. 'My father was a fisherman. I was born by the sea, in a little cottage on False Bay, not far from Fish Hoek. It seems to me that there was never a time when the sea was not a part of my life. How far back do your memories go, Kirby, and what do you remember? My own memories are all of the sea. My mother is in them, and my father. And there is always the sea.'

He stopped talking. Pablo had ceased his mad racing and had curled up at his master's side. Ross stroked him, an absent-minded sort of stroking, as if Pablo and the beach and the girl by the fire were far away, as if Ross was in a distant world where the girl and dog could not follow him.

Kirby was silent, her body taut with excitement. Ross had said when the moment was right he would talk about his life. When rapport existed. He'd said she would not need a note-book. He was talking now. And she needed neither note-book nor pencil. She knew that she would not forget a single word that came from his lips.

'One night there was a terrible storm. The lightning lit up the sea and the thunder seemed to bounce off the waves. My mother cooked the supper, but she herself could not eat. She kept going from the stove to the window. She put me to bed, and I remember that she seemed agitated. And then my father came home. His hair and his clothes were wet, and there was blood on his face. He came to my bed and looked down at me, his arm was around my mother who was weeping. I must have been about three at the time. It was only years later that I understood how frightened she'd been that night. The trawler had run aground on some rocks, my father was one of the survivors. That's my first memory, Kirby.'

As if the first memory had unleashed others, Ross went on talking. His father had taught him how to fish, first on dry land, later from a boat. Fish were a necessity of life, providing the money that kept the family clothed and housed in good times, almost the only food on their plates when times were bad. Never was there a doubt in the minds of Ross and his father that the boy would become a fisherman. His mother, worried sick too often by the dangers and uncertainties of the life, ventured the opinion sometimes that perhaps he should follow a different career, but even she did not entertain the thought seriously.

'How did you feel about it?' Kirby asked into a new silence.

'Good. I loved the ocean. I was on a boat any time I was given the chance. My father, my uncles, one of my grandfathers, had been fishermen. It was the natural path for me to follow.'

'No wonder you live by the ocean. You've loved it all your life.'

'Not all my life.'

Kirby was startled by the sudden harshness in his tone. Was it her imagination that his face looked more rugged than usual, and that his jawline was tight?

'No?' she asked tentatively, when it seemed that he was going to remain silent.

'There was a time when I hated the ocean. Loathed it. When I wanted never to see it again.'

There was a story here, Kirby sensed. Something that had meant a great deal to Ross in the past. Looking at the hard closed face, she wished she knew how far she could probe.

'I left Cape Town, left the sea,' Ross said. 'I travelled. I worked where I could. As a logger in Canada. A stint in construction in Peru. Once I worked as a chef in a seedy but rather wonderful restaurant.'

'Where you learned to make curry.'

'Don't you remember? I learned that from my

friend in Fish Hoek.' But it had been the right
thing for Kirby to say—a touch of lightness had
returned to Ross's voice.

It seemed safe now to say, 'But you came back.'

'As you see. I realised that my love of the ocean
was stronger than the hate. That I couldn't live
happily away from it.'

Kirby took hold of all her courage. 'Something
must have happened, Ross . . .'

'Yes,' he said very briefly, and threw a piece of
wood on the fire.

Wisely she kept silent this time. There had been
a crisis in Ross's life, and she'd give much to know
what it was. Hopefully he would open up to her in
time, but it would not be tonight.

At least they had made progress. Ross was
talking to her.

And once started, he went on talking. Mainly
about his life as a fisherman. Kirby learned how
Ross and his father would leave Fish Hoek before
dawn, how they would sail their boat deep into the
waters of False Bay. Sometimes the pickings were
meagre, but at other times they were good, and the
boat would return at sunset laden with snoek and
snapper and kingklip. Gulls would hover above
the boats, hoping for pickings, and holiday-makers
would crowd around them as they came in,
excited, curious to see the fish that would be in
markets and fish-shops and hotel-kitchens by the
next day.

'Superstition and tradition played such parts in
our lives,' Ross said. 'In my father's and
grandfather's days even more so. Then there were
the horse-drawn carts that would take the fish into
Cape Town and the suburbs, racing so that the
fish would stay fresh. There were the annual

quayside services, do you know about them, Kirby? How well I remember them. Clergymen of every religion took part. There were prayers to ensure the safety of the fishermen and the quality of the catch. We never missed them. It's only recently they've stopped having them.'

On the dark beach, with the only light coming from the tiny fire, Kirby listened absorbed. Ross's voice was low and vital, his words were evocative. A picture emerged of a young boy whose life had revolved around the sea, around fishing and harsh realities, so that a good catch meant sufficient for the day, and a series of bad days could herald disaster. Not a sad picture, however, for there was nothing in the telling to suggest that Ross had been in any way unhappy.

As he spoke Kirby tried to visualise the boy he had been then. It was hard to imagine him as a boy. There was something so strong and self-sufficient about the man, that it seemed if he must always have been the way he was now. But that was the stuff that fairy-tales were made of. No, the young Ross would have been almost as tall as he was now, but very slender, without the whip-cord hardness and muscularity of the man. There must have been times when he was frightened, when he wondered if a sudden storm would ground the boat as his father's boat had been grounded in his earliest memory. Times when he was lonely and beset by insecurity, when he lay in bed listening to the howling of a storm, hungry because the day's catch had been so poor that there was no money for food.

Kirby wondered about his family, about his friends, about school. Questions churned in her mind. There was so much she wanted to ask him.

Most of all, she wanted to know how the fisherman had become an artist of international repute.

'When did you start painting?' she asked, when eventually Ross fell silent.

'We'll leave that for another time,' he said. 'Are you cold, Kirby?'

Now that he'd asked the question she realised that she was in fact cold. Until this moment she had been so absorbed in his story that she hadn't even noticed the drop in temperature.

'A little,' she admitted, and wished she'd lied. It was so lovely out here on the beach, putting up with a bit of cold was preferable to going back to the house and her room.

'Soon remedy that,' said Ross. He put some more wood on the fire, and then he moved behind her. Before she had time to realise his intentions he was cradling her body with his own, his legs outstretched on either side of her, his arms enfolding her.

For just a moment she let herself enjoy the feel of that hard body against hers, around hers. Then she tried to move. 'Ross . . .'

'Nice isn't it,' he said.

His mouth nudged away the fall of her hair, and nuzzled her neck. She closed her eyes, thankful that he could not see them. They would betray the treacherous emotions she would give anything to suppress.

'Ross . . . move away please.'

His only response was to hold her more tightly, his legs clamping her body, his arms beneath her diaphragm. She could feel the tips of his fingers just gently touching the lower swell of her breasts.

'Ross, please . . .'

If only he would let her go. She should be able

to get away from him herself, of course, it wasn't as if he was imprisoning her with any force of any kind. Not physical force at least. But he was imprisoning her all the same, the force he used sensuous and deadly, robbing her of the strength to push herself away from him.

'Are you still cold?'

She was burning hot. Where her body was in contact with his, it was on fire.

'No,' she said, 'I'm not cold. Ross, why don't you respond when I talk to you?' Her voice was firmer now.

'I am responding. Though not perhaps in the way that you think you would like.'

He was right, of course. Her mind, the seat of reason and logic, wanted one thing. Her body, a mass of more needs and sensations than she'd ever realised she possessed, wanted something quite different. Her body was dominating her mind at this moment—though she'd never admit it to him.

'You think you know it all,' she said in a tight voice.

'There are things I know,' he said very softly.

With his body still cradling hers, he shifted over on the sand, just enough so that he could reach her face with his lips. His mouth was cool, but the sensation he aroused on the area beneath her ear was erotic. Kirby went rigid as she felt a sudden hunger in her loins.

'Stop it!' she burst out.

But Ross, it seemed, was a man not easily discouraged. He drew her back against him, so that she was lying with her hips across his thighs, and her upper body against his chest. Bending over her, he began to kiss her again, gently at first, and then with increasing passion, teasing her lips with his, probing with the tip of his tongue, driving maddened fire through her nerve-stream, sending all rational thought from her mind. Taking her with him to heights where she could no longer resist him. She opened her mouth to him, and felt him heave a sigh. Then he was kissing her even more hungrily, his mouth dropping kisses on her cheeks and her throat and her eyes before returning to her lips. His hands were moving too now. Kirby was not even aware that he had pushed up her shirt until she felt his hand on her breast.

Once more she went rigid, and Ross, sensitive to her every movement, was conscious of her tensing and his fingers stilled a moment.

'Relax,' he ordered softly.

'I can't!'

'Try, little one. I promise I won't hurt you.'

Somehow he reached the clasp of her bra, and then he was at her breasts once more, caressing the soft curves with the palm of his hand—a roughened palm, which had an eroticism all of its own, calling to something primitive and intensely female in Kirby, filling her with a hunger so deep that it seemed to rob her of all her defences. She tried to tell him to take his hand away—she really did try—but the words never made it out of a throat that had gone so dry that it was difficult to swallow.

His fingers went to her nipples. The big fingers were gentle yet tantalising in a way she would not have thought possible. The fire burning inside her was almost out of control now as she felt her nipples harden into his fingers, communicating her feelings in a way that he would never hear from her lips.

'I want to look at you,' he said huskily.

'It's dark . . . And you know how I look . . .'

'I want to see your body. We'll put more wood on the fire.'

He moved away from her to get at the wood. She'd been wrapped in the warmth of his body but now the cold air hit her—and restored her to sanity at the same time.

'No!' she said loudly. 'We're not going on with this, Ross.'

He did not answer as he put the wood on the fire. The fire flared, and he came back to her, but this time Kirby was ready for him. Her shirt was tucked back in her trousers, her arms were wrapped around herself.

'No, Ross,' she said tightly.

He dropped the hands that were reaching for her. 'You really mean that, don't you?'

Thank heavens he could not know that she meant it on one level only. She'd be lost if he did, for he had only to touch her for her to lose her strength of will.

She swallowed on the raw throat. 'I really do.'

'Why? We were both enjoying it.'

She pulled her knees up to her chin. 'I don't go in for this kind of thing.'

'This kind of thing, as you call it, is sex.' His voice was dry.

'As if I didn't know.'

He was quiet a moment, as if he was puzzled by the bitterness in her tone. 'Sex isn't a dirty word, Kirby. Not when it's something natural and beautiful between two people who are attracted together.'

'That's male sweet talk,' she said, thinking that he was not all that different from Jimmy. He was just a man—any man—after sex.

'At twenty-two you must know better. We all need to make love, Kirby.'

'Go on calling it sex.'

'I wonder why you're so bitter.'

She gave a casual shrug. 'I'm not bitter.' Heaven forbid that he should learn the truth. 'This type of thing is just not for me, that's all.'

'It's for all of us. You're no exception.'

He reached out a hand to touch her cheek, only to drop it when she flinched and drew away from him. For a while they sat in silence. The little fire crackled, the flames leaping and falling. The waves that broke on the rocks roared ceaselessly. Beyond the fire there was darkness, an intense darkness on all sides. Kirby still sat with her knees drawn to her chin, her eyes fixed on the fire. She was not looking at the flames at all, she was just keeping her gaze averted from Ross.

'Tell me about him,' Ross said at last.

Her breath jerked. 'Him?'

'The man. The one you meet on weekends.'

She relaxed in relief. 'What do you want to know?'

'Do you make love with him?'

'Is that all you think about?'

'I'm just interested,' Ross said mildly.

'No,' she said. 'We don't make love.'

'What do you do then?'

'I don't believe this! It's the most ridiculous conversation.'

'What do you do with him, Kirby?'

What did people do when they weren't making love? 'We go to the beach. We walk, go to concerts, to movies.'

'But no lovemaking.'

'There doesn't have to be sex.' She used the

word deliberately. 'Two civilised people can enjoy doing things together without sex.'

'Of course,' he agreed. 'But it has to enter the picture somewhere, otherwise it's a sterile relationship. What's his name, Kirby?'

Name? She nearly said 'Jimmy' because at that moment it was the only name she could think of. 'His name doesn't concern you,' she said loftily. 'I'll tell you this, Ross, his mind is on higher things than sex. Not that I expect you to understand.'

Ross gave a shout of laughter. It was a vital sound on the dark salty air, and Kirby felt a new ripple of sensation flame through her.

'Damn right, I don't understand. Does your civilised man have milk in his veins?'

'I won't have you talking about him like that.'

And now, because beneath the gentle veneer Ross was a very self-assured male whose pride had been dented, he would tell her that he could talk about her man any way he liked. She wouldn't be hurt—could one be hurt by an insult to a non-existent lover?—but she would be angry.

But Ross did nothing of the sort. In fact he said nothing at all. His silence lasted so long that Kirby, stealing a glance at the shadowed profile, wondered if he had lost complete interest in the conversation.

The flames were beginning to die once more. If they were to stay here much longer the fire would need more wood, but Kirby was darned if she was going to be the one to do anything about it. From not too far away came the barking of baboons, reminding her of the barren wilderness of the mountains and their proximity to the sea. The tide was coming in fast now, each wave climbing the slope of the sand just a little further than the last.

Soon the water would cover the very spot where they were now sitting.

'I suppose we should go back,' she said at last.

'Not yet.'

'The fire's dying and the tide is coming in.'

'You're running, sweetheart. What is it that makes you want to run away from things?'

The endearment was meaningless, and yet it shook her. 'I'm not running from anything.' She tried to make her voice firm.

'I don't believe your man doesn't want to make love to you.' His voice was low and vital in the darkness. 'You're a lovely woman, Kirby, a man would have to be abnormal not to want you.'

She was trembling, not just because he'd touched on the subject of sex again, but because of what his words implied. Ross found her desirable. Or was that just empty talk? Anyway, it was becoming more and more dangerous to remain in his company. She put out a hand in a token of protest. 'Stop analysing, please . . .'

'I've just begun,' he said.

'Well, you'll have to go on without me.' Jerkily she got to her feet, not caring at that moment that the beach was dark and unfamiliar, that baboons were not far away. Wanting only to get back to the house, to her room.

'You are running,' he said softly, and reached for her hand.

She stood unresponsive beside him, stiff and unhappy. And then he was tugging at her hand, showing her that he wanted her to sit down again. 'I won't hurt you,' he said. 'I promise I won't hurt you.'

It was the soothing quality in his tone, more than the words he used, which made her give in. Though an inner voice cautioned her for a fool.

An arm went around her shoulders, drawing her to him—gently—and then with the other hand Ross touched her cheek.

'You promised!' The words jerked from her throat.

'I promised not to hurt you, and I meant it.' His fingers were moving, trailing a path along her face, around her eyes and her nose and then her mouth, as if he was memorising her features.

'What are you trying to do, Ross?' It hurt to speak over the fires in her body which she was trying so hard to extinguish—with no success whatsoever. 'Don't you understand that I'm hating this?'

Liar. Wretched liar.

'You're not hating it. You're frightened, that's all. Why, Kirby, why?'

His tenderness was her undoing. 'I can't talk about it,' she choked.

'You don't have to. Just relax, darling. Let me love you. I'll show you just how good it can be.'

Oh, treacherous body. It should have been so easy to move out of his arms, he wasn't holding her tightly. Just a simple message sent from the brain to the muscles. But as before, when Ross began to caress her, she was totally incapable of sending messages of any kind. It was as if her brain was able only to deal with sensations, with nerve-ends that tingled as if they lay exposed at the surface of the skin, with the fires that were ignited in all parts of her.

'You're trembling,' Ross said.

'With repulsion.'

For a moment he stiffened against her. Kirby seized the advantage. 'That upsets you, I suppose.'

Incredibly, he laughed. 'It just makes me more determined to teach you what you should know.'

'Even if I can't bear it.'

'If I believed that I wouldn't go on with this.'

'Believe it!' She sounded a little desperate.

'I believe that you're frightened. That once you see what it can be like you'll enjoy it.' His voice roughened. 'Your body was made to be loved, Kirby.'

'You sound like a chauvinist,' she flung at him over the thundering in her ears.

'I don't mean to. I'm not about to exploit you, Kirby.'

Something in his tone got to her, keeping her silent. She was able to see Ross in a different light from other men. He was out for the fun he could get, yes, but he was also genuinely concerned about what he saw as her fear. He really wanted to help her. And he did not know that his help was the last thing she wanted.

'Ross, please . . . No . . .' She tried to move away from him, but the arm on her shoulder tightened a fraction.

'Relax,' he said, still with the same gentleness. 'I'm not going to rush you, Kirby.'

Lightly, very lightly, he brushed her face with his free hand. No man had ever used this feather-light touch on her before. Not Jimmy, not any of the others who had tried so hard to step into his shoes. Always there had been passion, and haste, and greed. Jimmy's first thought had been to find pleasure for himself—that she had enjoyed their lovemaking too had been an added bonus. The other men had been no different. Oh, they'd tried to woo her with wine and chocolates and fine dinners, but always she'd known what the quid pro quo at the end of the evening must be. And had resisted.

With Ross it was less clear what she was resisting. Earlier on he had been trying to get pleasure for himself. Now he seemed to be thinking only of her. And that only added confusion to the fire and the hunger already raging inside her.

His hand moved beneath the fall of her hair to cup the slender swell of her throat, his fingers moving on her skin with a lightness that might have been meant to reassure, and which merely succeeded in being erotic. The hunger inside her was a pain now, and she sat very still, praying that she wouldn't give herself away by an unconscious movement toward him.

'Not too bad, is it?' She heard the words against her hair.

'It's . . . it's okay.'

She felt the laughter in his throat. 'Well, that's a beginning anyway.'

He drew her closer, so that her head lay against his chest. She felt so snug, nestling in the angles of his body, her shoulder in the curve of his arm-pit, her head cradled between his chest and his chin, and the clean male smell filling her nostrils. Snug and safe, and terribly excited. All of them sensations for which she had no use.

He kissed her. A light enough kiss, giving no hint of his hunger which was there; she was sensitive enough to feel the tension in the hard body.

Closing her eyes, she gave in to temptation. She let herself imagine what it would be like to make love with him. To let herself go, to enjoy all that was in him to give, to give in return. To surrender herself totally to the sexuality and virility of this most attractive of men. The vision that presented itself in her mind was sensuous and wonderful.

Too wonderful. He was kissing her again, and her body was aroused and alive. Any moment now she would be turning to him, forgetful of all those decisions she had made. She would be unable to resist him. Their loving would be abandoned and passionate, and she would enjoy every moment of it, with no thought to the consequences.

But tomorrow she would wake to anger and self-contempt, despising herself for not having stopped when she could have. The game was not worth it.

'No, Ross.' She sat up, determination making her voice firm.

'You're still scared.'

Scared half to death, she thought grimly. Oh Ross, thank God you have no idea what you're doing to me. Or how hard it is to push you away.

'I suppose I'm not ready for it.'

'You will be,' he promised her, making no effort to force her back into his arms. 'In time you will be.'

He might just be right about that, she thought, as she stood up and brushed the sand from her jeans. Which was precisely why she was so very frightened.

CHAPTER SEVEN

On her pillow, after she'd breakfasted alone the next morning, she found another sketched portrait. Whatever else Ross was, he was no respecter of privacy. Amused, wary too, she picked it up.

Yet another Kirby. Hair loose this time. Something tremulous in her face. Something fragile and uncertain and yet sensuous in her bearing. A woman scared of loving, but wanting it too.

Through the tension mounting inside her, Kirby wondered how he did it. The uncertainty, the doubts and the fears. The hunger. Just a few pencil strokes, yet it was all there. Ross was a genius. The world had said so often enough, Mr Anderson had confirmed it. One did not have to understand geniuses, it seemed. But to live with one was disconcerting.

'I look beneath the mask,' Ross had said. When had she given him permission to look beneath hers?

He was in the studio, probably painting. The door was closed, and she had the feeling that he must have started early. He'd be there for hours, she sensed, and was glad. She was in no mood to be with him. She felt fragile and edgy, an echo of the portrait. Evidently Ross was not inclined to talk about his life this morning, and the last thing she wanted was to hear about it.

She would spend some time writing. Ross had given her something to work on, though of course there would have to be a lot more. So far he hadn't touched on his art. She wondered what had happened, and when, to make him hate the ocean. And who was the girl on whom he'd modelled the lovely copper piece? So many questions. But at least she could make a start.

Where to write? In his study? On the patio or on the beach? Best to have one place to work, and that place was surely the study. But she realised suddenly that today she could not bear to be anywhere near the house.

She felt so shaken, so restless. That first night, when they'd listened to Chopin and Ross had insisted on sitting close to her, touching her—that had been bad enough. Last night had been infinitely worse. Her mental well-being was mangled. For it to be healed she had to get away.

Asking no questions, she got into her car and took the road away from Cape Town to Hout Bay. She'd always understood why artists and poets flocked to the picturesque village—it was just the place if one wanted to feel inspired.

Writing-pad and pencils in hand, she wandered around the village a while before strolling down to the fishing-harbour. Hout Bay was not only a place where artists came to live and paint, it was also one of the hubs of the fishing industry.

It was filled with movement and colour. A fishing-trawler was putting out to sea, from another trawler men in denim overalls were unloading a catch. Everywhere there were holiday-makers. They thronged the harbour, looking at the fish, or waiting for a boat that would take them for a spin out to sea. On the pavement, not far from the harbour, sat two tribal women, gentle-faced and clad in long cotton-print dresses, the wares with which they hoped to tempt tourists spread out in front of them—hand-woven baskets and brightly beaded bangles and necklaces. The throats and arms of the women were adorned with beads, and Kirby stopped to admire them, knowing that each intricately designed necklace had a meaning—often a message or story of love.

The air rang with the sound of the sea-gulls. They squabbled over dead fish on the quays, and swooped low over the boats and over the heads of the holiday-makers. The gulls were the constant, Kirby thought, smiling. They were always here. As was the Sentinel, the mountain that rose straight and stern at the outer edge of the bay, keeping a constant watch on the harbour.

On a bollard near the water's edge Kirby sat down and opened her pad. Yesterday she'd put down her impressions of Ross's house, had tried very hard to describe the man—who seemed to defy description. Now she began to write about his life. About the little boy who was born by the sea, about the man who still had the need to live close to it.

Page after page she filled with her neat writing. At length she looked up and gazed around her. Thoughtfully this time. Hout Bay, the home of artists and fishermen. Ross—artist and fisherman. The place and the man. Was it coincidence that had brought her here today? Or was it something more profound, some prompting of her subconscious mind that had propelled her? At some level of her being was she thinking of Ross, even when she was not aware of it? The idea was disturbing.

She was doing a job. An assignment. She would do it carefully, would give it everything she could. But not to the extent that her mind became enslaved, obsessed by the man she was writing about. Never that!

Frowning, she went back to her work. For half an hour longer she wrote. But now she was troubled. She wanted to write with the detachment of an observer, yet she felt anything but detached. In her mind she could see the trawlers coming back to Fish Hoek at sunset, could see the young Ross with the catch. She had only to look around her to be able to see that other bay on the other side of Table Mountain where he had lived. On one hand it was very good that she could see it so vividly, and yet on another it was not good at all. For Ross's story, told to her by a dying fire on a dark beach, had stirred her profoundly. And she didn't want to be stirred by him.

Perhaps, after all, it had been foolish to come here. Discipline was what she needed to do the book; it was a discipline she would find at the desk in Ross's study. No matter if the sea and the fishy smell and the squawking gulls of Hout Bay gave her a clarity of vision that she would never have in the study. True, she owed it to the readers of the biography to give them a good picture of the artist they revered. But she owed it to herself not to destroy herself in the process.

Back at the house on the rugged cliff, she found that Ross was still closeted in his studio. Today it was going to be lunch alone—who knew whether Ross stopped to eat when inspiration took him?—and frankly, she was relieved. The less time she spent in his company the better. And if that was illogical—how was she going to learn about his life if not from him?—well then, at the moment she didn't feel very logical.

Kirby's lunch was a cup of coffee and a slice of the delicious *melktert* left in the fridge. Afterwards she went to the study to go on with her writing. But there was a limit to what she could write. When she'd set down all she knew of Ross's life, she felt restless once more.

Still no sign of him as she emerged from the study. She was on her way to the patio when she saw the painting, and she knew it was only because there were so many other treasures in this house that she hadn't noticed it before.

A Ross Dolby. Even without the signature she'd have recognised it. There were the colours, the strong lines, she'd come to associate with Ross's work.

But there was also something more. She stared at the painting, her eyes as fixed to the canvas as if they were magnetised, and she felt something moving inside her. Something wild and tumultuous.

She didn't try to define what it was that moved her so intensely. The picture was of the sea. A stormy sea, with a solitary gull tossed helplessly on the boiling foam of the waves. As subjects went, it was not unique, you had only to go into any art-gallery in Cape Town, and you'd find all the seascapes you could want. What made it different from any other picture she'd seen was the treatment, the merciless merging of lines and shapes, the angry slash of paint. There was *feeling* in the picture—a feeling that corresponded, somehow, to the turmoil that raged inside the woman who stood riveted before it, unable to move.

In those moments it didn't matter that it had been painted by Ross. She hardly gave Ross, as the artist, a thought. The only reality was that here, in this picture, were echoed emotions which tore at her, and to which she could give no name.

She was not thinking at all as she touched it, her finger sliding lightly, then hungrily, over the paint.

'Do you like it?'

Kirby jerked her finger from the painting, and whirled around. 'I didn't know you were here.' The words were painful in her dry throat.

'You haven't answered the question.'

She stared at him, her face ashen.

'Well, do you like it?' The words were casual enough, but his eyes were intent, as if he wondered at the extremeness of her reaction.

Kirby found her voice. 'It's not pretty.'

'You find it ugly?'

'In a way.'

Nothing in his expression changed. 'Then you don't like it?'

'I didn't say that!'

He took a step towards her, and she knew he saw that her eyes were wet. 'Kirby ...'

'Yes, Ross! It makes me want to cry. But I don't know why ...'

Something seemed to move in his throat. 'Touch it.'

'No!'

'You were touching it when I found you.'

'Yes ...'

'Touch it, Kirby.'

Still she did not move. She flinched when he reached, quite suddenly, for her hand, and propelled it towards the picture.

'Touch it,' he said again. 'Don't be scared, Kirby.' His voice was gentle.

He was still holding her hand, and now she did

not fight him. She let him guide her, let him move her fingers over the thick paint, tracing the lines of the picture, *feeling* it.

'What do you feel?' He was speaking so quietly now, it was more like a whisper.

'I ... I can't say.'

'Yes, you can,' he insisted, so close to her that she felt his breath, warm as a summer wind, on her cheek.

Still she tried to evade him. 'Nothing. There's nothing.'

'That's not true, Kirby. I can see it in your eyes, and it's not just the tears. Kirby, tell me. Tell me what you feel.'

She spoke then. The words torn from her, dredged from the very core of her being. 'There's rawness. Loneliness.'

She stopped. Ross remained silent. There was just the big rough hand on top of hers, the paint beneath it.

'There's hunger. And sadness. And a wild passionate joy.' The words just came from her throat. She couldn't stop them. She didn't think about them. If she had thought, she would have clammed up. But she was beyond thought.

'All the things you feel yourself,' Ross prompted softly.

'No!' The word burst forth violently. And then, as her eyes fixed on Ross, 'I don't feel any of those things. None of them!'

'I think you do.'

What had she given away of herself? Appalled, she stared at him, knowing that in the space of a few seconds, when she'd been beyond thought or reason, she'd shown him a glimpse of her soul.

The hand that had been holding hers left it, as

both his hands came up to cup her face. Big hands, so big that they encompassed all of her face, from the pointed chin over her cheeks and ears, reaching to the sensitive area above her eyes.

Ross said, 'You try so hard to create an image, Kirby. A pretty picture-postcard girl. Efficient and cool.'

'Don't go on, please don't go on.'

'You're not like that at all.' There was a sense of wonder in his voice, even though it was Ross who'd said from the beginning that she was not the woman she pretended to be.

There's hunger in you, Kirby. And passion.'

Her eyes were wide and green and she could only look at him wordlessly.

'There's sadness,' he said, 'and I wish I knew the reason for it. But there's also a marvellous capacity for happiness.'

She didn't want him to go on, but she seemed helpless to stop him.

'You've got it all wrong,' she said at last.

He didn't try to contradict her. 'Do you want the picture?' he asked.

Such a thought had never occurred to her. But now that he'd asked the question, she knew that she'd give all she owned to possess it. If that painting hung on one of her walls she'd never want anything else.

Reality hit. 'I could never afford it. I don't have that kind of money.'

'It would be a present.'

Incredulous, she stared at him. 'You'd give it to me?'

'Yes.'

'But it must be worth an absolute fortune.'

'Perhaps.' He smiled at her, the smile that did

such nerve-tingling things to her senses. 'You've given me something too, Kirby.'

'What?' she asked unsteadily.

He'd never looked at her like this before. He was so very close to her. His hands were still cupping her face, and though it was their only point of contact she was nevertheless aware of every long hard inch of him. There was a warmth that seemed to flow from him into her. He had stopped smiling, and there was a strange tension in his eyes. A tension that was repeated in every part of her body. He was going to kiss her, And it was what she wanted. No matter how much she might try to tell herself otherwise.

But he didn't kiss her. 'I'll tell you on the day I give you the picture,' he said.

He dropped his hands then, and stepped a little away from her. Kirby knew she should have been glad. But she felt utterly disappointed and bereft.

They had *sosaties* for supper that night. Kirby prepared them with unusual care, tiny cubes of lamb alternating with onions and green pepper on long skewers which Ross *braaied* on a fire at the side of the house. 'Very good,' he said, when he'd taken a bite.

'As good as the curry?'

'Well ...' He pretended to think. 'Yes, reluctantly I have to say yes.'

Kirby laughed softly. After the intensity of the afternoon's emotions, it was a relief to be able to joke together. She didn't know whether Ross had been affected by the scene with the painting. She did know that up until a few minutes ago she'd felt raw. Even now, she still felt drained and exposed.

'What shall we eat tomorrow?' he asked, and she laughed again.

'Do you ever think of anything but food?'

'Seldom,' Ross said very gravely. 'Do you?'

Their glasses were filled with a delicate Riesling, a wine which had been made not far away, in the lush Paarl valleys beyond the mountains. They talked lightly, casually, neither of them touching on the things that were uppermost in their minds. Around them the crickets shrilled, and now and then from a nearby *krans* there came the sound of the barking that sounded like dogs but had to be baboons.

Afterwards they walked on the beach. In the west, the sky was a brilliant mass of colour, in the east the sea was already shadowed. A south-easter, the warm summer wind of the Cape, ruffled the tops of the waves.

'Why would anyone not be on this glorious beach tonight?' Kirby remarked.

'Why indeed.'

Ross was close beside her, his steps matching her own. Now and then his arm or his leg brushed against her, casually enough, but each time the contact sent shock waves trembling through Kirby's system. It was as if, now that her body had started to respond once more to a man, it was making up for lost time.

'Actually,' Ross said lazily, 'I'm glad we have the beach to ourselves.'

She glanced at him quickly, then away, hoping he hadn't noticed the sudden colour in her face. Ross would be a fool if he did not know by now that he affected her, and Ross was nobody's fool. The thing was not to let him know the extent of it.

He reached for her, and she tried to pull away from him, but he wasn't trying to kiss her—he was taking the pins from her hair.

'Why did you do that?' she asked a little unsteadily, when he ran his fingers through it, almost as if he was combing it.

'Because I wanted to.'

She tried to instil some indignation into her tone. 'Just like that.'

'And because I will not talk to you about myself when your hair is up.'

'No notebooks or pencils, that was the condition.' She looked at him, and thought how incredibly handsome he was with the wind ruffling his dark hair, and the sun gilding his tan and turning it to copper. How could any woman be unaffected by him?

I never had a chance, she thought. Right from the beginning I never had a chance to resist him. And now it may be too late.

He laughed. 'Did I say it would be the only condition?' His hands were still in her hair, and now she felt his fingers on her throat, stroking the sensitive skin with a sensuousness that threatened to drive her right out of her mind.

'You're a bit of a rogue,' she said, and he laughed again.

'Perhaps I am. You really want to talk, Kirby?' And when she nodded, 'All right then, we'll talk.'

He dropped his hands, and she knew that once more she was disappointed.

'I stole my first paints,' Ross said, as they walked on.

'You did *what*?'

'You look shocked. Have I gone down in your estimation, Kirby?' He looked amused.

'I'm not here to judge you. Just to record.'

'Heavens, you've gone prim on me again.' He stopped walking and cupped her chin in one of those big hands. 'I think you do it purposely to annoy me.' His eyes sparkled as he looked down at her. 'So you're shocked. I suppose he wouldn't have stooped so low, that hero of yours?'

'Never,' she defended the non-existent man in her life—not an easy feat when she was trying her best to stop herself laughing back at Ross.

'Does he have no vices?'

'None that I can think of.'

'How do you put up with him?' The wicked fingers were on her throat again, seeming to know with unerring certainty just where to excite her.

'Perfection may be good for the soul,' he said, after a few moments, 'it's a bore for the beholder.'

'Maybe so.' Kirby refused to let herself rise to the bait. 'But my friend's not under discussion—*you* are.' She smiled up at him, willing herself not to let him see how much he was exciting her. 'Why did you steal paint, Ross?'

For a long moment he looked down at her, his eyes penetrating, yet enigmatic. It was a gaze that lingered on her lips and her throat, lazy, yet with just a suggestion of insolence. Kirby felt her heart beating faster.

'I was six years old,' he said.

'You knew you wanted to be an artist even then?'

Ross grinned. 'What I wanted was a bicycle.'

He dropped his hand. Kirby had a mad urge to reach for it, to put it back against her throat. Where it seemed to belong.

She asked, 'Did you get it?'

'An art competition, that's what it was. No set subject. The prize was a bicycle. I wanted that bicycle more than anything else in the world.'

He was smiling, as if at the memory. She

registered the sensuousness of his lips, the whiteness of his teeth against the rugged tan. Ironic, she thought. At last Ross was talking, and she should be hanging on every word, yet all she could think of was that for sexuality he would be a hard man to match.

Briskly, she said, 'And so you stole a box of paint so that you could enter the competition?'

'Right. The boy's name was Billy, and he had more toys in his room than I'd seen in the window of the toy-shop in Fish Hoek. I don't believe he ever knew the paints were gone. I painted a picture of—what else?—the sea and a fishing-boat.'

'And you won the bicycle.'

'No. The judges thought it was an awful painting. I know, because in my disappointment I went and asked them.'

Compassion stirred inside her for the disappointment of a little boy who'd wanted a bicycle so much that he'd had to resort to stealing to win one.

'Little did I know then,' Ross said, 'that life plays games its own way. I didn't get the bicycle. What I did acquire was a love of painting.'

'That's when it started?' Kirby was fascinated.

'Way back then, yes. With a stolen box of paints, and a painting that other people thought ugly.' He ran a hand through his hair. 'If I'd won the bike I'd have been off riding it every minute I had. I didn't have a bike, but I did have a box of paints.'

Another grin, the roguish one this time. 'I was not the sterling stuff your hero seems to be made of, Kirby. Once I had the paints, I wasn't about to give them back. I did another picture, and then another. It was like a drug, once I'd started I couldn't stop.'

A lump formed in Kirby's throat. 'I think that's beautiful,' she said softly.

'Prim Kirby abandoning her principles?' he mocked, but the hand that went to her cheek and caressed it was seductive.

'How did your parents feel about it?' she asked, pretending to ignore his touch.

'My dad didn't care either way. He didn't see it as a threat. My mother was a gentle soul, sensitive, and she was pleased. She encouraged me. She even saved her housekeeping money and bought me paper.'

Kirby was silent a while. At last she said, 'So when you were six years old you knew you wanted to be an artist?'

'Nothing like that. Art was my pleasure. My way of expressing myself, though I doubt I could have thought of it in those terms myself. It was my way of finding happiness when times were bad.'

'When did you know it would be a career?'

'Not until years later. I've told you I was a fisherman. I fished for years, with no thought that I'd ever earn a living any differently.'

'Something must have changed your mind.'

'Something did.' Said in the same tone he'd used yesterday, when he said there'd been a time when he had hated the ocean.

Kirby was silent, waiting for him to explain. But he didn't. Silently they walked along the darkening beach, and Kirby found that she was having to quicken her pace because Ross had quickened his.

But there were things he was not ready to tell her. Might never tell her. Things she wanted so much to hear. Not just because of the book, she realised, in a revelation that surprised her just a little. She wanted to know for herself. She felt as if she wanted to know everything about Ross that there was to know.

Presently he went on talking. He told her more about his childhood. About a dedicated teacher who had recognised his talent and encouraged it. About a young people's art exhibition, and a judge who had given him a prize. About his first sale, when a honeymoon-couple from the Transvaal had watched him sketching on the pier in Fish Hoek, and the young bride, wanting a memento of the honeymoon, had begged her husband to buy the picture.

Now and then Kirby asked a question, or inserted a comment. Mainly she listened. With the ear of the ghost-writer who would write his story. With the emotions of a woman who found herself thinking about the man more and more.

How right he'd been when he'd said she would need no notes of what he said. As Ross spoke she could see the things he told her, felt as if she was living some of the scenes with him. If he had dictated the details of his life, there would have been a flatness. Something would have been lost in the telling.

As it was she knew that she would forget nothing he'd said. Knew too that there were other things she would remember. Things that would never appear in the book. The excitement of being near him in the dark, listening to him talk. The tone of his voice when he was reminiscing. The smell of damp seaweed. The feel of cool sand as it filtered through her toes. The touch of his hand when he steadied her on a patch of slippery rock.

More than anything she would remember how it had been to feel like a woman once more, with the emotions and passions of a woman. It was a memory that would hurt, for she'd forgotten none of her principles even if, temporarily, she was in the grip of a craziness so that she was not able to live by them. She would remember Ross and the feelings he had aroused in her long after she had left him.

And she knew—she was afraid—that she would miss him more than was good for her.

It grew dark, and still they were on the beach. The darkness didn't seem to bother Ross. He knew every inch of the coast-line for miles on either side, he didn't need a light to show him the way. Kirby was not worried either. Ross knew what he was about, and with Ross she felt safe. If anything, she was sorry when they turned back in the direction of the house. She could have walked with him all night, and never grown tired of it.

I'm a little mad, she thought. I'll have to leave him one day, and then I'll be sorry I let him get to me like this. But even that sobering thought did not detract from her enjoyment.

They were entering the house, and Kirby was about to say good night, when Ross reached for her. In a reaction that had become automatic, she stiffened, but he put a finger across her lips before the words of protest could emerge.

'Relax,' he said very softly. 'Please, Kirby, relax. Just enjoy it.'

He'd closed the front door, and now he leaned against it as he drew her towards him. She could feel every inch of the long hard body, could feel how much he wanted her. But as always he was surprisingly gentle. His kisses were tender, exciting her without frightening her. That was it—he was trying very hard not to frighten her. He didn't know that his very tenderness was erotic, creating a hunger deep inside her.

One arm supported her back, the other hand moved on her hair, her face, brushed her throat. And all the while he was kissing her, more tantalisingly now, yet still gently. He wasn't forcing a response from her, he was arousing it. With success. The hunger grew, her body felt as if it was on fire. She wasn't fighting him—there was nothing to fight. She was fighting herself. The hands that craved the joy of exploring him, the body that would have arched towards his if she hadn't concentrated on keeping it rigid.

There had been women in his past, she tried to remind herself, there would be other women in his future. This was just a man's way of enjoying himself, and oh Lord, she knew all about that. But then she felt his hand on her breast—when had he removed her clothes? And there was nothing she could do to prevent the hardening of her nipples, or to stop the torrents of desire that drove all rational thought from her mind.

Almost convulsively, she put her arms around his back and parted her lips. She felt the sigh that shuddered through him, and then he was kissing her again, more passionately this time, and all she could think of was that the sweet clean taste of his mouth was a sheer joy, and that she never wanted him to stop kissing her.

When he lifted her into his arms and began to carry her across the dark hall-way and down the passage that led to the bedrooms, she made no move to stop him. Her eyes were closed, and her head was against his chest where his heart was beating as hard as hers, and her arm was around his neck—not because she was frightened that he would drop her, but because she needed to be close to him.

He carried her into his bedroom, and put her down on his bed, bending with her, never breaking contact with her as he lay down and gathered her to him. And then he was kissing her again, and she was kissing him back with all the ardour of a woman aroused.

She didn't stop him as he continued to undress her. Indeed she helped him, lifting herself from the bed so that he could reach the buttons of her blouse. And she waited, trembling, as he removed his own clothes.

His naked body was warm and vibrant as she melted against him. His shoulders and his back were smooth, and her hands moved with the movement of his muscles. He began to caress her once more, and it was sheer joy to feel his fingers follow the curves and swells of her breasts. And then his lips followed the same path, and the breath seemed to stop in Kirby's throat as she arched against him.

His head lifted. 'You're so lovely,' he said raggedly. 'Kirby darling, I want you. I want you so much.'

Only as much as she wanted him. She had never wanted anything as much as she wanted him now.

He was looking down at her. It was dark in the room, but the curtains were open and there was some moonlight. Her eyes had become accustomed to the darkness, so that she could see his face.

'I won't hurt you,' he promised.

'Ross . . .'

Love me, she was about to say. Please, love me.

But she didn't get the words out, because Ross was saying, 'It will be fun, darling. Fun.' And suddenly she knew what she'd done. What she'd allowed him to do.

With a small cry, like that of an injured animal, she pushed herself from the bed, remaining in the room just long enough to snatch up her clothes before she fled through the door.

'Kirby! Kirby, stop!'

She didn't wait to hear what he said as she ran out of the house into the night.

CHAPTER EIGHT

Ross caught up with her on the path that led down to the beach. She'd heard him shouting of course, 'Kirby! Kirby, come back!' but she'd taken no notice. She just went on running, stumbling on the unfamilar path, pausing only long enough to pull on her clothes before continuing with her headlong dash.

His arm shot out, catching her round the waist, and she would have fallen if he hadn't steadied her.

'Crazy woman,' he raged. 'What are you playing at? I looked for you on the patio, never thought you'd be fool enough to come down here in the dark. What's with you, Kirby?'

She couldn't answer him. Her shoulders were heaving, her whole body was trembling. Tears choked her eyes and her throat. She just stood in the circle of Ross's arms—a most unloverlike hold this time—and thought how *good* it was to be close to him, and how impossible everything had become.

'Well?' he demanded.

Still she didn't answer, but she put her hands to her face, covering her eyes where the first tears were threatening to fall.

'Kirby. Kirby . . .' His tone was suddenly gentle. Heart-rendingly gentle. He'd registered her distress, and was distressed himself. 'What's wrong, love? I didn't hurt you?'

'Oh, no,' she said through her fingers.

'You're repulsed by me?'

She shook her head. Even in her distraught condition she heard the uncertainty in his voice. Strong, self-assured Ross was uncertain. Oh Ross, she thought, Ross, Ross.

'The fellow in Cape Town. He means so much to you that you can't bear me to touch you?'

Had she been in a more rational state of mind she might have taken her opportunity and lied. But she just shook her head again. 'It's not that.'

'Then what is it? Kirby darling, I knew you didn't want to make love, but I wanted to show you how good it could be. What fun . . .'

The endearments warmed her, even though she knew they meant nothing in themselves, that it was just the way he would speak to any woman who was upset.

'Did you hate it so much? Was it something I did?'

I loved it! I adored every moment of it. I felt I never wanted it to end.

She dropped her hands from her face and looked up at him. She'd never met a man who valued her own pleasure as much as his. She owed him something.

'It was nothing you did.' Her voice was ragged with tears. 'Anyone else would have enjoyed it.'

'We're not talking of anyone,' he said savagely. '*You*, Kirby, *you*. What wasn't right about it for you?'

'You said it was fun . . .'

'That was what got to you? The word "fun"?' She could feel him looking at her in the darkness, studying her. Knew that his eyes would be penetrating. 'It's not fun for you?'

She swallowed. 'No.'

He was silent a few moments, and she wondered what he was thinking. He was no longer holding her, and she missed that. Almost she closed the tiny gap between them. But for once her mind won over the dictates of her body, and she remained where she was.

If Ross knew the thoughts going through her head he'd take her for insane, she thought wryly.

'I can't accept that,' Ross said suddenly.

'There are women who don't like sex,' she returned tentatively.

'I know that. And there's a reason every time.'

He was getting too close to the truth. 'Not necessarily.'

'We're not getting into that.' He sounded impatient now. 'I only know that you were enjoying it. You were, Kirby. You were responding.'

'Yes,' she said after a moment.

'Then you must have been enjoying it.'

There was no way she could deny it. 'Yes,' she said again.

'Then what happened? You have to tell me, Kirby, why is sex not for you?'

What would he say if she told him the truth? Just like that. But she couldn't tell him, not tonight, not ever.

'This is very difficult for me,' she said painfully.

'Why?'

When she didn't answer he touched her cheek, very softly, as if he was taking care not to scare her away again. She didn't move, and so he tucked a tendril of hair behind her ear. Still she didn't move. She was frightened to move. Inside her raged the twin fires of desire and frustration. All she could think of was how badly she wanted to go back into his arms, to shed her clothes, to make love with him.

'You're frightened,' he said at last. 'You're a virgin, and you're frightened of what it will be like.'

Well, in one respect at least he was right. Not because she wondered what it would be like to make love. She knew what it was like, though she also knew that she'd never experienced it fully. With Ross it would be wonderful. So wonderful that she could become addicted to it. And then she'd crave it long after Ross was beyond her reach. That was one of the things she was frightened of.

'You *are* frightened, aren't you?'

'Yes.'

He put his arms around her, still very softly, though she could feel the tension in his body and knew how much it cost him to be so restrained. She felt his lips in her hair.

'I won't hurt you,' he said softly. 'I'll see that it's good for you. Come back to the room with me, darling.'

'No,' she protested, too violently.

A new note appeared in his tone. 'You're in your twenties. A mature woman. You're awake to sex, I know it. Felt it.'

'It's not for me.' There was despair in her voice. 'Don't you understand?'

'I understand that you're very frightened. But this isn't a normal fear, Kirby.'

She didn't answer him. There was nothing left to say.

But Ross hadn't finished. 'Something's happened to make you so frightened. What is it, Kirby? Please tell me.'

He soon saw that she wasn't going to answer him. He drew her into his arms and held her. He was being so gentle. And she wanted so much more. Her heart was beating hard, and her body was one mass of burning awareness. If he were to make violent love to her here, on the path, she didn't think she could resist him. There was a limit to her control. She'd responded to him earlier, when he was kissing her, and she knew she'd respond again now—and this time there would be no stopping. She wanted him too desperately for that.

But Ross didn't know it. He held her a long while, his arms around her, his body warm and hard against hers, his lips moving in her hair.

'I'll teach you not to be frightened,' he said presently. 'Not tonight, Kirby. We're both going back to our rooms, to sleep—though how I'll get to sleep God alone knows.' Just for a moment he couldn't keep the frustration out of his voice. 'But I'll teach you. You're not going to be frightened of love all your life.'

'Some people have all the luck,' Lynn said, smiling wryly. 'What wouldn't I give to be in your place.'

'You'd be welcome to it.'

On Kirby's lap was Meg, a sleepy little Meg after a day spent playing with her mother. Kirby gathered the small warm body closer against her, nuzzled her nose and her lips in the soft hair. How she had missed the little girl. Yesterday she had been hard put to concentrate on her writing, all she could think of was that in one more day she would be back with Meg. If Ross weren't so utterly stubborn she could be home with her every night.

'She looks wonderful,' she said now. 'You're a darling, Lynn, it's a relief to know she's in such good hands with you.'

'That's because I adore her.' Lynn was regarding her with compassion. She knew what the days away from Cape Town meant to her friend.

And then she said, 'Why do you hate Ross Dolby so much?'

Kirby looked at her. 'What gave you the idea that I hate him?'

'But you . . .' Lynn stopped and drew breath. 'My God, Kirby, you've fallen in love with him, haven't you?'

Kirby shook her head. 'Not love. With a man like Ross Dolby that would be a one-way thing. Besides, you know how I feel about it. I'm absolutely determined never to fall in love again.'

'Love has a way of happening,' Lynn said doubtfully.

'I don't believe that. It's not for me anyway. That's one trap I'll never get myself into again. I'm not even sure love really exists.'

Kirby looked down at Meg, then stared out of the window. The cloud hung thick and white over Table Mountain. From the harbour came the sound of a fog-horn.

Without looking at her friend Kirby said, 'No, I don't love him. But something has happened.'

'What?' Lynn was taut with suspense.

'I think I've fallen for him. It's just a physical thing, but it's sheer hell.'

'And he's ignoring you?'

'Anything but. He'd like nothing more than to make love. He's tried more than once.'

She looked at her friend, and now her eyes were wide with distress. 'It's like nothing I've ever

experienced. Jimmy ... Jimmy was just a boy,
Lynn. All the others, the men I've had dates
with—each one of them was just out for what he
could get.'

'And Ross?' Lynn prompted, when Kirby
stopped.

'He's so different. I wish I could explain.' She
made a little gesture with her hands. 'You'd never
take him for an artist, Lynn, I didn't. Tanned as a
sailor, rugged, and strong and self-assured. A real
man.' She paused a moment before going on in a
new voice. 'Tremendously sexual. But gentle too.
So gentle, you wouldn't believe it.'

'Wow!' Lynn said.

'Exactly.' Kirby sounded rueful.

After a moment Lynn said, 'You've fallen for a
dynamic man. He wants you. Sounds like heaven.'

Kirby lifted the sleeping baby, and put her down
on the sofa. Then she went to the window. There
was a view from here up to Devil's Peak, and that
was fairly clear though the great mountain beside
it was not. On the street a man was scattering
bread-crumbs to the pigeons.

Without turning, she said, 'It's not what I want.'

'Why on earth not? Oh, I know what you said
before you started working with him. But if he
loves you, and you ...'

'Who said anything about love?' Kirby swung
round quickly. 'I told you-it was just physical. I
don't love him, never will. And Ross doesn't love
me, Lynn. He could get any woman he wants, for
heaven's sake. He's rich, famous. Sexy. He can
have all the women he wants queueing up at his
door.'

'Does he?'

'Probably.'

Childish, Kirby thought. That sounded stupid and childish.

'You said he wants you,' Lynn said.

'What I said was that he wants to make love to me,' Kirby said heavily, a little sorry that she had ever started on Ross. Yet needing to talk about the confusing thing that was happening to her.

'And why not?' she went on at last. 'I'm there. Available, day and night. Alone with him miles away from his nearest neighbour. He wouldn't be normal if his mind didn't turn to sex. He's a man after all.'

'A moment ago you said he was different.'

'Yes . . .'

In body Kirby was in Cape Town. In mind she was back in a house on a wind-swept mountainside on the wild Atlantic coast. In Ross's bed. With Ross caressing her, arousing her to undreamed-of heights. 'He cares about the way I feel,' she said in a low voice. 'He sees that I'm frightened—and he's reached the wrong conclusion. He takes me for a virgin.'

She looked up at Lynn and her eyes were distressed. 'He's the sexiest man I ever met, the most passionate. But he's so tender too, and he doesn't know what that does to me.'

'You haven't told him about Meg then?'

'No! You see, while he thinks I'm a virgin he doesn't force me to go further than I want to go.'

'I understand, and yet I don't,' Lynn said softly. 'I get the feeling you're frightened of him, but I'm not sure why.'

'Because he wouldn't have to resort to force. That's why.'

'Kirby . . .'

'Yes, I'm frightened. Not of Ross, of myself. I

don't know myself any more, Lynn. Do you know how terrifying that can be?'

'He's wakened you.' Lynn's voice was warm with comprehension.

'With a vengeance! I didn't know I could feel this way. Excited. Aroused. Wanting to touch him. Wanting him to touch me. It's awful.'

'It sounds rather wonderful.'

'Someone else might think so.' Kirby looked distraught. 'I don't want to be involved with a man. Never again.'

'But you enjoy his lovemaking.'

'Too much for my own damn good. I really thought I could handle this sex thing, Lynn. That no man could ever make me feel again—unless I wanted it.'

'And it's not the way you imagined.'

'No,' Kirby said unhappily. 'Ross has made me aware of my sexuality.'

'You mean he's shown you that you're still a woman.'

'Yes.' She covered her eyes with her hands, as if she could not bear to face the truth.

At last she looked up. 'It's not what I want. It's not pregnancy I'm afraid of, I'm an adult now and I can take care of myself. It's something else. Remember we talked about it before I took on the assignment? Meg and my career—they're the only things that count in my life. That hasn't changed.'

'Could you ask your boss for a replacement?'

'I've tried. Besides, I want to write this book.' A little hopelessly, Kirby shook her head. 'I'll have to stick it out. And hope I come out of the experience with my sanity intact. God alone knows how I'll do it.'

With that, she walked over to the sleeping child.

'Now what shall we do tomorrow? I want to make the most of every moment I have with Meg.'

'Pleasant weekend?'

Kirby smiled. 'Very.'

'Good.'

Looking at Ross, Kirby realised that she was seeing a new aspect of the man she thought she knew. There was an aloofness in his face that she'd never noticed before. Something hard and remote. Though he'd expressed interest in her weekend, Kirby didn't believe that he cared one way or another whether she'd enjoyed herself. And that was as it should be, she tried to tell herself. No personal feelings entering what was a temporary business relationship.

'What are our plans for today?' she asked.

'I'll be painting,' he said coolly.

And I don't give a damn what you do with yourself, his tone implied.

I've missed him, she thought as she watched him walk away. And the strange thing is that I didn't even realise it. I was so busy with my darling Meg that I didn't know I was thinking of Ross—except for when I told Lynn about him. And all the time I was missing him.

But something had happened to Ross. Somehow, in the space of a weekend, a warm sensuous laughing man had been transformed into a remote stranger. It was clear that he hadn't given Kirby a thought while she'd been gone. Perhaps the few days alone had made him realise that he preferred not to have her around. Which only went to show how important it was not to let herself get emotionally involved with him.

She spent the morning in his study, writing. At

noon she made herself a light lunch, and afterwards she went on with her work. She didn't see him until supper, a silent meal, for Ross seemed preoccupied.

And so Kirby was surprised when he said they were going for a drive. Ross didn't say where they were going, and his strange mood persuaded her not to ask.

It was already dark when they took the coastal road to Cape Town, a road that wound so sharply around the edge of steep cliffs that people who'd had even one drink were advised not to attempt it. Ross was still silent, and after a look at the unusually tight profile Kirby changed her mind about trying casual conversation. Rolling down her window, she breathed in the fresh sea air and made an effort to calm herself. She was feeling tense, and she knew why—Ross had something on his mind, and his mood was affecting her.

Everywhere there was darkness—the mountains on one side, the sea on the other, with only the strong head-lamps of the car to light up the road. And then, in the distance, appeared the first lights of Cape Town. Strung along the coast-line, climbing the lower slopes of Table Mountain were the lights. Vanishing and re-appearing with every twist and turn of the road.

Kirby glanced at Ross, but still he was silent. Mystery man, she though grimly. Well, if that was the way he wanted to play the game she wouldn't give him the satisfaction of showing her curiosity.

They had passed Llandudno, the village dark and brooding on its finger of land stretching into the sea, and now they were in Cape Town's outlying suburbs, Camps Bay and Clifton. Just when Kirby thought they were driving into the city itself, Ross turned off the main road and put the car into low gear for the climb up the mountainside.

Kirby knew where they were of course. Ross was taking the road that went up Kloof Nek to Signal Hill. She knew the road so well, but it never failed to thrill her. Up they went, higher and higher around the Nek. Below them were spread the lights of the city. Towering above them was the awesome buttress of Table Mountain.

This was a drive for young lovers. On summer evenings they came up to Signal Hill to be alone. Kirby wondered why Ross had brought her here. Not because he needed a dark private place for some stolen kisses. His house above the wild sea had all the privacy any couple could want. Nevertheless, her heart beat a little faster.

At the top of Signal Hill he brought the car to a halt. Again Kirby looked at him. And saw that there was nothing remotely lover-like in his expression. If anything, his face was taut.

'Quite a sight,' she commented, trying to keep the nervousness from her voice.

'We didn't come here to see the lights,' he said harshly. 'Or to cuddle.'

She was glad that he could not see the warmth that had come into her cheeks. This new Ross had her confused. Something must have happened to bring on this mood. Something she had done? She rejected the idea. She had done nothing wrong.

'What did we come for then?' she asked quietly.

'To talk. That's what you want from me, isn't it? All the lurid details of my life.'

She did not know how to act with this strange Ross. And so she remained silent until he chose to talk again.

'There were three of us in the family,' he said at last. 'A brother, a sister, me. John was ten years older than me. He had gone to sea by the time I'd stolen that first box of paints.'

His voice was hard. Impersonal. He sounded as if he were reciting facts he'd read in a textbook rather than memories of his life. And again Kirby wondered—why?

'Annie was two years younger than me. We squabbled, as children do, but we were very close. We complemented each other, I suppose. Annie was soft, sweet. I was something of a young hellion. Annie loved to watch me paint. She'd sit by my side hour after hour watching. When I tried portraits she was my first model. As for me—when I was painting I would ignore her, but I was very protective of her. Savagely so. My first fight—and there were plenty in those early years—was because of Annie. A boy at school had hurt her. Somewhat of a cliché, I suppose, a brother beating up a child who'd hurt his young sister. But this is *my* life we're talking about. *My* sister. I was only eight at the time, but I hit that boy so hard that he needed a couple of stitches in his head.'

He stopped speaking. He wound down his window, and stared out over the carnival of lights, though Kirby doubted he was actually seeing them.

Ross was back in Fish Hoek, with his family. With his sister. With memories that meant more to him than any he had recounted thus far. Kirby was so tense now—without quite knowing why— that she found it hard to breathe.

'Annie and I did things together,' he went on at last. 'Swam, surfed. Looked for mushrooms in the

Tokai forests. Spent a summer picking grapes near Paarl. One thing we never did—we never went out in a boat together. My mother had a thing about it. She'd seen too much. Had been worried too often. It was enough that the men in the family spent their lives on the sea. Annie was not to go in a boat.'

Inside Kirby the tension was mounting. She didn't know what was coming. She just knew, intuitively, that she would rather not hear it.

Ross was so close to her on the seat of the car. Only a few inches separated his thigh from hers. Once, when he moved his leg, it brushed hers, and the all-too familiar tingling shivered through her. But he hadn't noticed the contact at all, of that she was certain. In spirit he was not in the car on Signal Hill. He was in another place, another time. He spoke his memories aloud, and yet Kirby felt sure that he was hardly aware of her presence.

He was silent again. Longer this time than before. When he started to speak once more, his voice was even harder than Kirby had heard it. Harsh, cold. Painful to listen to.

'I'd been fishing for a few years. Painting in my spare time, earning my living at sea. One day Annie asked me to take her out in the boat. She'd asked me often, always I'd refused. That day she pleaded. Mom and Dad had gone into Cape Town. We were alone at home. What the hell—nobody would ever know. I gave in.'

Ross looked across the seat at Kirby. 'You know what's coming, of course. I'll tell you anyway. There was a storm. Blew up out of what I'd thought was a blue sky. If there were storm clouds I didn't see them. At least not in time to get back to shore. I don't have to tell you what a storm at sea can be like. The boat tipped over. We were both flung out. I managed to hold on. I couldn't see Annie. I kept shouting her name. There was no answer, I wouldn't have heard it anyway over the sound of the thunder and the waves. I just hoped like crazy that she was holding on too. She wasn't.'

'She drowned?' Kirby whispered painfully.

'Her body was found a few days later. On a beach miles up the coast.'

'Oh, my God!' Kirby stared at Ross numbly. She was trembling. Her throat was so choked with tears that she could barely swallow. Ross's expression was hard as steel, yet vulnerable too. So vulnerable that she felt she was invading his privacy by looking at him. She turned her head, not only to hide her tears, but to look away from Ross.

A hand seized her wrist, gripped it, cruelly. 'What's the matter?' Ross rasped. 'You wanted to know about my life. Is it too much for you?'

Numbly she shook her head.

'Does it embarrass you to see a man spilling out his guts?'

'I'm not embarrassed. Just sorry. So very sorry.'

'Sorry's a meaningless word. People say it all the time.'

Ross. Poor, poor Ross. Her heart went out to him. She longed to close the space betwen them. To draw his head to her breast. To give him some of her warmth and comfort. And knew she could not do it. It was not what he wanted.

'You're right,' she said instead. 'What I should have said was that I grieve for your pain.'

'Yes.'

'I can't even begin to understand the pain. How did you go on living?'

Ross drew a long shuddering breath. But when he spoke his tone had lost a little of that impersonal hardness. 'For a long while I didn't. I thought of suicide. Does that shock you, Kirby?'

'Go on.' She kept her voice as neutral as possible.

'I realised in the nick of time that it would solve nothing. But I was like a crazy man, Kirby. Mom and Dad's grief to contend with. My own. My terrible guilt. Always knowing that if I hadn't given in to Annie's pleading, it wouldn't have happened. I couldn't sleep, couldn't eat. All I could do was paint. I painted and painted. I did nothing but paint. Ugly pictures, you'd have hated them. But they were my release. I painted all my grief, my guilt, my feelings of worthlessness.'

'You said once there'd been a time when you hated the ocean.'

'That was it, of course. I left the sea. I felt I never wanted to see it again, live near it again. I did all sorts of things. Travelled. Picked up whatever work I could find. And all the time I painted. My art became my lifeline.'

'But in the end you came back.'

'I came back, yes. And became a full-time artist.'

It might have been the wrong question to ask, but she asked it anyway. 'If the accident hadn't happened—do you think you'd be where you are today?'

Incredibly, Ross gave a small laugh. 'That's the question I've asked myself a thousand times. Would I still be a fisherman? Would I have become an artist? I can't give you an answer, Kirby. I don't know.'

This time it was Kirby's turn to be quiet. In a weak moment Ross had given in to his sister's pleading—and now he was famous when he might not have been, otherwise. In a weak moment Kirby had given in to a man's pleading, and now she had a daughter she would not have had. And she knew that she could no more think of life without Meg than Ross could think of his own life without his art.

She turned and found him watching her. 'The lovely copper girl . . .' She saw Ross tense, but she went on. 'She's Annie?'

'Yes. A copper piece. It was all I could do—I couldn't give her back her life.'

Ross seemed more relaxed, as if by talking he'd released some of the tension that had threatened to explode inside him. I want him to hold me, Kirby thought. I want it so much.

And she did what she'd never dreamed she'd do. She moved across the seat and leaned her head against his shoulder. If Ross was surprised he didn't show it. He slid his arm around her, and as she rested her cheek against his chest he caressed her arm with a rough hand.

I'm mad, Kirby told herself. But just for tonight I don't care.

After a while she said, 'You're usually so cheerful. A stranger would think you'd never suffered pain in your life.'

'It's in my pictures. You picked it up, do you remember, Kirby?'

The painting in the passage. The one she'd touched. *Felt.* Oh yes, she remembered.

'We all have our pain, Kirby, and we have to go

on.' He was looking down at her. 'I wonder, have you learned that yet?'

She stiffened. Grew rigid. She was about to pull away from him. And then she let herself relax. 'I'm learning,' she said.

CHAPTER NINE

In the weeks that followed Kirby had much to write about, for now that Ross had told her about Annie's drowning it was as if the last barriers to talking had been torn down. Whenever Kirby thought she knew everything about this fascinating man, there was more.

She also had time. Their routine had changed somewhat. Ross had an exhibition coming up, and though he still did a fair amount of painting, many was the day that he had to drive into Cape Town. He came back late then, sometimes just before sunset. Kirby, who had all the hours and privacy that she could possibly want, often found time hanging heavy on her hands.

The worst thing possible had happened. She was actually *missing* Ross. Not that she needed him constantly around her. What she missed was his presence in the house. Well, she'd tell herself, when she was finally conscious of the drift of her thoughts, one of these days he'd be out of her life, the only memory of the man would be a book on the shelf in the apartment. Might as well get used to missing him now—then it wouldn't be so hard later. And with a kind of fierce determination she'd get back to her work.

Though she told herself every day that Ross had no place in her life, she was touched when he told her she was to come with him to the opening of the exhibition.

He looked amused. 'You seem surprised.'

'I am a little.'

'You must have known I was expecting you to come. An opening is always important. Good heavens, Kirby, you're a part of my life.'

Stupid, stupid heart that it should beat faster. 'Temporarily,' she acknowledged lightly.

His jaw tightened just a little, but the smile remained in his eyes. 'Of course,' he agreed.

In a way, she really was a part of his life—temporarily. It could hardly be otherwise the way they were living. What she hadn't expected was how well they would get on together. Their worlds, their experiences, their backgrounds, were all so different. Yet they found themselves laughing at the same jokes, enjoying the same music (when it wasn't loud trumpets), relishing their long after-supper walks along the lonely beach, discussing the portraits which still found their daily way to her pillow.

Above all there was—face it—a sexual attraction which never waned but only grew stronger. Kirby had long ago stopped pretending to herself that she felt nothing for Ross. She did feel. Time hadn't lessened her awareness whenever she saw him, the tingling nerves and the beating heart when he touched her. But neither had it changed her resolve. The book was getting on well, the time to say goodbye was drawing closer every day. She would *not* allow herself to be destroyed by the parting.

And so when Ross made love to her, she tried very hard to keep a part of herself detached. No matter how much she yearned to let herself go fully, to yield to her own sexuality, she drew on all her strength to maintain her reserve. Amazingly, Ross was as patient with her as he'd been at the beginning. She sensed his frustration, but he never gave way to it. She remembered the night he'd promised to rid her of her fears—to all intents he was still trying. She wondered sometimes, wryly, what he would do if he knew that his frustration was only matched by her own.

'Stay with me this weekend,' he said now.

She looked at him startled. Weekends were sacrosanct, he knew that. 'No, Ross, I can't.'

'We've had so little time to be alone together lately.'

Her heart turned over at the expression in his face. If he knew how badly she wanted to be with him he'd be amazed. But Meg was more important to her than Ross. Meg would be a part of her life long after Ross had become a memory. There was no way she would give up the precious two days with her child.

'He's so important to you, that fellow?'

There were times when Kirby regretted the day she'd invented her wretched lover. But he was useful too.

'Yes,' she said firmly.

'I see.'

There was a grimness in Ross's face. His eyes were hooded, unreadable. It was time to change the subject.

'I've never been to an opening. What do I wear?'

'Any damn thing will do,' he said with uncharacteristic impatience. 'I wish women wouldn't keep worrying about their clothes.'

'I expect I'll find something,' Kirby said diplomatically.

She had hit a sticky patch in the book and there was something that needed clarifying. She'd intended to sit down with Ross, now, but she sensed he was not in the mood for it. As she went back to the study she wondered about his abruptness. He must know that she had a life of her own apart from the hours that she spent with him. His impatience—had she glimpsed anger too?—was unreasonable.

The days immediately before the exhibition were hectic. Kirby abandoned any attempt at writing and helped Ross instead. Many a trip was made to Cape Town. There were quick words and frayed nerves, and sometimes Ross looked haunted.

'You'd like to stay on the rocks fishing while the exhibition runs its own course,' Kirby teased.

That drew a laugh from him. 'How well you know me,' he said, and touched her cheek. 'I've never been an exhibition man. They're a necessary evil in an artist's life, but oh, how I hate having to dress up in a suit, having to be nice to people.'

Both of which he did extremely well, Kirby decided, as she stood a little to one side and watched him on the day of the opening. His dark suit, superbly cut and expensive, emphasised his height and the breadth of his shoulders, and he wore it with elegant ease. I've never been able to imagine him in anything but denims, she thought, but he looks dynamic, more distinguished—and sexier—than any man in the room.

Around him swarmed his fans, well-dressed, well-groomed people, champagne glasses in hand. Mainly women, Kirby noticed. They hung on his words, they touched his arm, many were openly flirtatious. If Ross meant what he'd said about hating having to be nice to people he was certainly hiding it well. He was laughing, attentive, responsive by turns, and the flirtatiousness didn't seem to bother him a bit.

I couldn't be jealous, Kirby thought. That would be awful.

Not knowing a soul in the room, and having no fund of small-talk, she felt a bit awkward. She stood nursing a drink, and trying to look relaxed, and was glad she'd gone to some trouble with her own clothes. Since that first day, when Ross had coaxed her out of what he'd laughingly termed her 'professional image clothes', she'd spent her time in slacks and sundresses. For today she had chosen a silk sheath in lovely merging shades of emerald and turquoise. It was a simple dress, carefully chosen with an eye to both fashion and economy, as were all her clothes. But it clung softly and seductively, making the most of a slender figure. On her wrist was a heavy gold bracelet, in her ears a pair of antique ear-rings, jewellery which had belonged to her mother.

Ross had been talking for some minutes to three very well-dressed women, when he caught Kirby's eye and beckoned to her to join them. Courteously he made the introductions. Kirby said 'How do you do,' and tried to smile, but it was hard to get the smile to reach her eyes when the women looked at her with such unconcealed curiosity.

'Miss Lessard *lives* with you?' The woman who asked the question was wearing a wedding-ring, but she looked as if she could quite cheerfully have used her well-manicured nails to scratch out Kirby's eyes.

'I'm doing some research on Mr Dolby's life,' Kirby said, her voice carefully expressionless.

'Finding out all about my dark and wicked past,' Ross grinned.

'Preparatory to ghost-writing a biography.'

It was stupid to resent the way he joked with the women, stupid to be angry because he seemed so obviously to enjoy all the attention they were lavishing on him. But then lately she seemed to be stupid very often in situations that concerned Ross.

'So you work for a publishing company,' said one of the other women, and there was something in her tone that set Kirby's teeth on edge. You're only with Ross because that's your job, seemed to be the implication.

'Tell us about the book, Ross,' came the plea. But he laughed, and said they'd have to wait till it was published, they could read it then.

The conversation went on, the topic changing from the book to the exhibition—'the pictures are adorable, Ross, better each time'—to people. Names which Kirby knew only from the newspapers were bandied about. There'd been a cocktail party here, an opera première there. These women had been everywhere, knew everybody. And Ross knew all those people.

But Kirby did not. It must have been obvious to all concerned that she did not know one of the people they spoke of, that all the talk of divorces and re-marriages and this one going abroad with that one, meant absolutely nothing to her. Still the conversation continued. Kirby felt an outsider. She *was* an outsider. Whereas Ross belonged. With these people. In this gallery. She was sorry she had agreed to come to the exhibition with him.

'Excuse me,' she said with sudden relief, when she spotted her boss. She had been hoping Mr Anderson would be here. She'd never really thought of him as a friendly face, but that was what he was now.

No small-talk necessary now. He was eager to hear how things were going, with the book, with Ross. Kirby told him all he wanted to know. Well, not quite all, but enough. And all the while a part of her remained detached from the conversation. She was looking at Mr Anderson, but she was seeing Ross, watching him flirt, and inside her anger was boiling up into a fine temper.

'Genius,' observed her boss, when he'd seen the paintings. 'The man's a genius, Kirby. I told you it pays to humour him.'

'Only up to a point,' she said grimly, wondering what Ross would do if she went up to him and wrung his tanned neck.

'You've managed splendidly.' He was smiling. 'And I'm not the only one who thinks so. Heard of Dennis Demayne, Kirby? Right—the fellow who's achieved such a name for himself in the music world. We've been after him for some time for a biography. I showed him what you've done thus far on Ross, and it's possible he may want you to work with him next.'

'Oh, really?'

'It would be a real break-through for you, Kirby. Ross Dolby and then Dennis Demayne.'

'It would be wonderful,' she agreed, but her voice lacked enthusiasm.

She hoped Mr Anderson did not pick up the tone she'd been unable to control. It was absurd, totally absurd, and yet she was unable to keep her eyes away from Ross. Here she was, being offered a boost up her career ladder, and all she could do was resent the way those women were fawning on Ross.

'We'll talk again when you've finished this assignment,' said her boss. 'Will you excuse me, Kirby—there's someone over in the corner I must talk to.'

It was a long hot evening, but it came to an end

at last. For a man who hated exhibitions Ross seemed in a good mood. And why not? Seven paintings sold at astronomical figures. A commission to do a painting for the foyer of a new bank building. Two art critics whose written reports should be glowing if they in any way resembled their verbal compliments.

'Another opening over,' Ross said, as they got into the car. He had taken off his tie and jacket and unbuttoned the top buttons of his shirt. 'Enjoy yourself, Kirby?'

'It was a riot,' she said brittlely. She was hot and tired and ready for bed. She could not wait to get home.

And then she saw that the mountain was on the wrong side of them, they were not going home at all. She sat up straighter and looked at Ross.

'We're going to Fish Hoek.' He turned his head and grinned at her, his teeth glinting white and strong in the darkness.

'At this time of night?'

'There are times when I feel like getting back to my roots.' The grin intensified. 'Seriously, though I'm much too wound up to think of bed. The heat was hellish in there. I just feel like getting on to the beach.'

'I know of a beach nearer home,' she said with some asperity.

'But I feel like a swim. So we're off to warmer waters, Kirby.'

She was not surprised to find that he'd brought a casual change of clothes for them both. Nothing about Ross surprised her any longer, not even the fact that he'd gone to her room and rummaged about for a shirt and some jeans without so much as a by-your-leave. They changed in the car, in the dark, where nobody could see them. And then Ross took Kirby's hand and they ran down to the beach.

'Do you have swimming-trunks?' she asked.

'Ever tried skinny-dipping?'

'You don't mean that?' she said. 'You're really crazy, Ross.'

'Crazy enough to have brought a bit of laughter back into your voice?'

So he'd noticed her tension. Did he also know the reason for it? And yes, Kirby decided, he did mean to go skinny-dipping.

Well, he wasn't the first one to try it, he wouldn't be the last. There was little risk that he'd be caught—it was very late and the beach was deserted.

'So much for the distinguished artist in the elegant suit,' she observed as he began to shed his clothes.

'You really hated the suit, didn't you.' His tone was enigmatic. But she had no chance to think about it, because he went on. 'You'll swim too, won't you, Kirby?'

At any other time her response would have been a quick and automatic refusal. But she was not her usual self-possessed self tonight. Some of the emotions that had burned in her at the gallery still lingered. The jealousy, the anger. Anger at the women who had treated her so superciliously. Anger at Ross. Anger at herself.

'What the hell,' she said.

'I take it that means yes.'

She could hardly draw back now. Nor did she want to.

The water was lovely. Warm, buoyant, the tide just right, not too low, not too high. Kirby was an excellent swimmer, and she knew these waters well. A wave was rising, and she dived into it. Anger and jealousy drained from her as she began to swim. After a while she stopped. It was too dark to see Ross, but she knew he'd be swimming too, and not far away from her. She swam a few yards shorewards, and then let the waves carry her.

On her bare body the moving water felt sensuous. Exciting. Kirby wondered why she'd never let herself enjoy this particular pleasure before.

'Nice?' a voice very near her asked.

She saw his head above the water. 'Very.'

'First time you've skinny-dipped?'

It was as if he'd read her thoughts. 'Yes.'

'But not the last. Let's do this often, Kirby.'

Spoken as if there was time in their relationship. Didn't he understand that they would be saying goodbye soon?

He came closer, and now his hands were on her shoulders. It was too dark to see his face. 'Still angry?' he asked.

'No.'

Her body was soft, yielding, as he drew her to him. He was able to stand but she was out of her depth and her arms went around his neck. For a long time he just held her against him and it was more exciting than anything she'd ever experienced, even with Ross. The waves that rose and fell. The salty darkness. And the two naked bodies, so close together, moving with the movement of the water.

By the time he began to kiss her, desire was already a hot tide of fire flooding through her. Always till now there had been some remnant of rational thought, however small, but not now. At the first touch of his lips her own parted, and she was kissing him too. The salty taste of his mouth was exciting, the feel of his wet body so erotic that she pulled herself closer against him, letting herself shape her body against his. We fit together, she thought exultantly, we were meant to fit together.

The hard body shuddered against her, and she knew that he was as aroused as she was. He was still kissing her, but not her mouth now. His lips had gone to her throat, brushing the long slender curve, and then he lifted her suddenly in the water so that he could kiss her taut breasts. He held her weightless body with one hand only now. With the other he was exploring her, caressing her, sliding his fingers from her breast to her waist, to her hips and her thighs.

And all the time she was making love to him too. Kissing him wherever she could reach him. Touching him. Committing the hard lines of his body to a memory of the senses. Never thinking, never regretting. Tonight was a night out of time. There had never been one like it, there never would be again.

'This is fantastic,' Ross groaned at last. 'But it's not enough.'

She knew what was coming and she was breathless. 'No.'

'Let me love you, Kirby.'

'Yes! Oh, yes!'

Still holding her tightly he carried her shorewards. Her heart was beating so hard that it felt as if it would burst right out of her chest, and there was not an inch of her body that did not throb with tension.

They came out of the sea, and he let her stand on the sand. Arms around each other, they walked to the spot where they had left their clothes. Ross had brought out the big towel which he always kept in the boot of his car, and he spread it over the sand.

Kirby stood watching him. She was trembling, every part of her was trembling. Ross straightened and came to her. He put his hands on her hips, clasping them, the fingers of those big hands spread wide over the smooth wet skin.

'I won't hurt you,' he said, with that exquisite control he'd managed to show every time he was aroused.

'I know that . . .'

'Kirby. Kirby, darling . . .'

She put a finger over his lips, shutting off the words. She was not afraid of being hurt. At least not physically, in the way that Ross imagined. Her fear stemmed from something else altogether, and it was drowned out tonight by an urgency which was greater than anything else. She knew it had been growing inside her all night.

'Make love to me, Ross,' she whispered. 'I want you to make love to me.'

His hands were still on her hips, but now he was drawing her against him, in a contact so erotic that she wanted to cry. Two wet bodies, both naked, wanting each other with a hunger that had been building in them for weeks—now, on this dark deserted beach there could be no stopping. And they both knew it.

He put her down on the towel, lay down beside her, and gathered her to him. 'You're so beautiful,' he groaned huskily. 'You're driving me out of my mind.'

And then, with a sudden snapping of that superhuman control, he let out a wild cry. 'You're so beautiful, Kirby!'

His first caresses were tender, but then a passion took over, and Kirby did not resist him. She was a woman aroused, and passion was what she wanted tonight. Every touch of his lips and hands made the blood sing more wildly in her veins. Her limbs were wet still from the sea, and yet they felt as if they were on fire. There was passion in her too as she made love to Ross. It was as if her body spoke its own language, one which only Ross could understand.

Nothing in her life until now had prepared her for this. Jimmy . . . An urgent but awkward boy. Jimmy's love-making had been a quick and fumbling thing. Ross was a man, passionate beyond belief, and yet tender, so tender, he considered Kirby's pleasure as much as his own.

When he lifted his body over hers, she was ready for him, every nerve clamouring for the release that only Ross could give her.

In the car, on the way home, Ross said, 'You'll stay with me this weekend, won't you?'

Kirby sat close beside him. She leaned her head against his shoulder. 'I can't.'

'I want you to.'

She looked up at him. From where she sat she could see the line of his cheek and chin. 'I'll be back Sunday night.'

'I don't want you to go at all. My God, Kirby, don't you understand?'

Some of the lovely languor ebbed from her limbs as she felt his body go rigid against her own. 'Ross . . . I do understand.'

'Then why?'

'It's something I have to do. We agreed at the beginning.'

He made a furious sound in his throat. 'Don't give me that! Surely tonight has changed things.'

Changed! It had turned her world upside-down. Shattered everything she thought she knew, everything she believed. None of which she could say to Ross.

'I really have to go,' she said slowly.

'Then our lovemaking meant nothing to you?'

Apart from Meg it was the most wonderful thing that had ever happened to her. On some distant rational level of her mind she perceived that tomorrow she might well be appalled at what had happened, especially at how very much it had meant. Not now though. She didn't give a damn. It had been marvellous—and that was all that mattered.

'It meant a lot,' she said simply.

'I tried so hard,' Ross said. 'All these weeks. I knew you were frightened of sex. I thought you must have been hurt. That someone had harmed you.' His jaw tightened, as if at a thought that had passed often through his mind.

'And then we made love tonight. And you seemed to be responding, Kirby.'

'I was.'

'I could have sworn you were enjoying it.'

Her throat was thick with tears. 'I enjoyed it, Ross.'

'I don't know if I believe it anymore. Not if you go.'

'I have to.' She stopped, searching for words. 'Cape Town ... The reason I go home for weekends ... It's nothing to do with this. Ross. With ...' She had been about to say 'us', but that could have been misconstrued, and so she said instead, 'With what happened. I just wish you'd believe that.'

'You're asking a lot.' His voice was cold and hard.

'Ross.' She pushed herself a little away from him as the last of the languor vanished. 'You're so angry.'

'Now why would I be angry?' he mocked.

But he *was* angry. The anger was there in the tight line of his mouth, in the hands that were clenched on the steering-wheel, in the increased speed of the car as it sped through the night.

'I think you're in love,' Lynn said. 'I've never seen you so radiant.'

'I'm not in love. I never will be.' Kirby smiled at her friend. She could actually feel the radiance Lynn spoke of. She had even seen it in the mirror, in newly glowing eyes and skin. 'But I'm happy.'

Lynn looked fascinated. 'You've slept with Ross, haven't you?'

'Yes. Oh Lynn, I was so certain I had no feelings left. Or if I did, that I could keep them under control. I kept fighting myself. I've had to learn that this is the way I am.'

'But no love?'

'No love.' Kirby shook her head firmly. 'Oh, I could never be promiscuous. Perhaps I'll never sleep with any man but Ross—it certainly couldn't be the same with anyone else anyway.'

'Don't you feel *anything* for him?'

'Of course I do. I like him more than any man I've ever met. I've enormous respect for his artistic vision, for his gentleness, for his sense of fun and adventure. You could say I like everything about him.'

'Sounds like love to me.'

Kirby smiled. 'I don't think I'm making much sense to you.'

'Very little actually.'

'I don't know if I can explain. Men have always known what it was to have sex without any strings, Lynn. Jimmy did. All those others who tried so hard to get me into bed on the first date. Why should women be different?'

'We are. *You* are.'

'Perhaps I'm not.'

'And perhaps Ross loves you.'

Kirby shook her head. 'Not Ross. He could have anyone. He's enjoying me, just as I'm enjoying him.'

'You're putting yourself down.'

'Just being realistic,' Kirby said drily, remembering the flock of elegant women at the exhibition, and the way Ross had relished their attention.

'What if he does love you?' Lynn persisted.

Kirby frowned. 'It wouldn't change anything,' she said after a long moment. 'Meg and my career. They are what matter. Even now.'

'I don't want to see you get hurt,' Lynn said uneasily.

'I don't see how I can be. I'm happy. Really happy for the first time in years.'

'And when the time comes to say goodbye?'

Kirby put her cup carefully down on the table. 'I'll have to face that when it happens.'

She got up and went over to Meg who was playing with a new doll. 'Meggie, darling. Mummy's taking you out this afternoon. Shall we go to the zoo?'

Meg's favourites were the monkeys. They were in a playful mood, swinging from branch to branch, catching one another's tails, stopping now and then to snatch the peanuts Meg threw through the bars of the cage. The little girl could not see enough of them, and the more outrageous their games, the more she laughed.

Kirby, who'd seen too little of her daughter in the weeks she'd been with Ross, had no eyes for the animals. She was looking only at Meg, revelling in the sound of her laughter.

'Having fun?' a deep voice asked.

Kirby spun round. Ross? It couldn't be! But it was. She stared at him in pure astonishment. What on earth was he doing here?

He was watching her, in his eyes an expression that she couldn't define. 'Enjoying the monkeys?'

She felt ill at ease. 'Very much.'

Ross was looking at Meg now. 'Pretty little girl.'

'She is, isn't she?'

'A god-daughter? Or a niece?'

'. . . Something like that.'

What was he doing here? Apart from sea-birds, Ross had never painted animals. Did he intend to give them a try? Somehow the explanation failed to satisfy Kirby. His presence here seemed just too much of a coincidence.

'How about some tea, Kirby? An ice-cream for the little girl?'

'Thanks very much, but I don't think so. It's time we . . .'

She wasn't able to finish the sentence for Meg said, 'Icy, Mommy. Icy?'

'Meggie, no,' Kirby said, her face flushed.

Ross looked dumbfounded. 'Mommy?'

'Icy, Mommy,' Meg said again.

Kirby knew a fervent wish to vanish from this spot, to be able to believe that none of this had happened.

'Why does she call you Mommy?' Ross asked harshly.

Meg clutched Kirby's hand. 'Don't like man.'

'Why, Kirby?'

He had a nerve interrogating her like this! Defiantly Kirby lifted her head. 'Because I am her mother.'

Ross's face was a mask. Hard, cold, unreadable. Kirby looked at him, and felt angry and slightly ill. She would explain of course, but not in this public place. Not in front of Meg.

'Ross . . .' She stopped. She wasn't sure what she wanted to say.

And then it didn't matter after all. Because Ross, his face still hard and cold, was walking away from her.

After a sleepless night Kirby drove away from Cape Town. Her mind was in a turmoil. It was really silly to feel so overwrought. All night she'd seen the dreadful mask that had come over Ross's face. Yet now, in the light of a new day, she was able to tell herself that what she'd seen was pure shock and astonishment. What she had to do was tell Ross the truth—which she should perhaps have told him long ago. Ross was as tolerant as he was unconventional. He might wonder why she'd kept the truth from him, but he would understand.

He was in the studio when she arrived at the house a little after ten. Normally she left him well alone when he was painting, but today—well, today was a little different.

She opened the door of the studio, and saw him at his easel. She said, 'Ross,' and went towards him.

Only to stop when he turned, and she saw his face. Something in his expression made her blood go cold.

'Ross,' she said again, uncertainly this time.

Pointedly he looked at his watch. 'Aren't you late, Mrs Lessard?'

'I didn't know I was expected to clock in. And it's *Miss*.'

'Miss?' One eyebrow had lifted.

Tolerant Ross. Understanding, tolerant Ross. Stupid Kirby. Why had she thought this man would be different from all the others?

She lifted her chin in a challenge. 'Miss. Do I have to spell it out, Mr Dolby? M.I.S.S.'

'So it really is Miss Kirby Lessard after all,' he mocked.

Kirby didn't think she had ever been quite so angry. Or so disappointed. 'Of course.'

'The frightened virgin who wasn't frightened or a virgin.'

'Don't,' she said, her voice very low.

'And who is the father of the child?' he asked conversationally. 'Or have there been so many that you don't know?'

If she'd felt ill yesterday, now she felt really sick. 'Stop this, Ross! Please . . .'

'Please, Ross. Stop this, Ross. Where I have heard those words before?'

She hadn't thought she could hate him. But she hated him now. 'That meeting yesterday. Was it coincidence?'

'Of course not. I wanted to know who it was you were meeting. I followed you.'

'How could you!'

His jawline was hard and cruel, his eyes filled with the unfamiliar mockery. 'I didn't think of asking your permission. I don't intend to ask for it now.'

As he flung down his paintbrush she knew what

was coming. Blindly she made for the door, but he moved more quickly than she did.

The kiss was hard, punishing. Kirby hated it. She kept her lips tightly closed, her body rigid. It was a brutal kiss. Mercifully it lasted no more than a few seconds.

Ross released her as abruptly as he'd taken hold of her. Kirby took a few steps away from him. They faced each other, both pale, both breathing fast.

And then Kirby turned on her feet and made for the door. It didn't take very long to pack her things and carry them to the car. Long enough though for Ross to come and apologise. To try to stop her. He did no such thing. When she walked through the house for the last time she saw that the door of the studio was still closed.

So this then was farewell. It was certainly not the departure she had imagined.

CHAPTER TEN

A DAY later Sally was installed in Ross's house. Before she went Kirby gave her the notes she had made, the copy she had written. It hurt to hand it all over. Not that it should. Just words and paper, she tried to tell herself. Things hadn't worked out, that was all, it would be silly to let herself get upset over it.

But she *was* upset. Not that upset was the right word for what she was feeling. She tried to hide her pain with a smile. But that didn't stop it from wrenching and tearing inside her. If emotions could bleed, then Kirby's were bleeding.

'What happened?' her boss had asked on her return to Cape Town.

'A personality clash.'

'Things seemed to be going so well.'

'It did seem that way I suppose. But ... We weren't hitting it off together, Mr Anderson.'

Don't ask me any more. Please, don't ask me any more. I'm not sure if I can answer without crying, and I don't want to cry.

Mr Anderson looked at her thoughtfully, but his only comment was a 'Hm.'

Later in the day he said, 'About Dennis Demayne. It will still be a while before he'll be ready for you.'

'Oh ...'

'So it's back to proof-reading for the meanwhile.'

She was grateful for that. She'd been wondering

166

if Mr Anderson would want her back in the office
after her precipitate parting with Ross. She had
been wondering how she was going to support
herself and Meg if he did not.

'Must seem a little routine after working with
Ross,' Lynn commented that evening.

'Routine can be merciful.'

'Want to talk about it?'

Kirby looked across the table at her friend, saw
the eyes that were warm and friendly and
compassionate. Lynn knew how she'd felt with
Ross. Knew she was hurting. And she wanted to
help. If she was curious too, well, that was only
natural.

'Eventually,' she said after a moment, and her
voice was subdued.

'That's fine. Any time you need a sounding-
board, just say the word.'

Kirby tried to force a smile. 'Some time soon I
may take you up on that. At the moment I'm still
too raw and bruised.'

Lynn made a little gesture. 'Is he worth it?'

'No man is worth it,' Kirby said feelingly. 'I'll
get over this.'

And with that she changed the subject.

It was strange, but lovely, to come back home
after work each night to be with Meg. It was
strange being at the office again, working to a set
schedule. But though she'd thought it would be
easy to pick up where she'd left off, it wasn't easy
at all.

Kirby found she had to concentrate very hard
on her work, because if she didn't her mind quite
automatically went back to the house on the cliff.
Without being aware of what she was doing, she'd
find herself thinking of Ross. She would see him at

the easel in his studio, or on the patio with a beer, or on the rocks with his fishing-rod. And then, with a kind of mental bang, she'd realise the drift of her thoughts, and try to jerk herself out of them. And that was an unbelievably difficult thing to do.

The nights were the hardest. Long after Meg was asleep, Kirby would lie awake. It was very hot in the flat, and when she could stand the sleeplessness no longer she would go and stand on the balcony and look up at Devil's Peak or down over the sweep of lights to the ocean.

Thank goodness she hadn't fallen in love with Ross. Now, when it was all over, she acknowledged how close she'd come to it. It was no satisfaction to know that she'd been right all along to keep her emotions detached.

'I thought he was different from other men,' she said once, painfully, to Lynn.

'And he isn't . . .'

'In many ways he is, of course. But Lynn, I began to believe in him. I thought he would never hurt me.' She was silent a few moments. 'Jimmy hurt me in one way. Ross in another.'

'Do you think perhaps you should try talking to him?'

'About what? His attitudes? I could have sworn I knew him, Lynn. He was so tolerant, so unconventional, that was the Ross I thought I knew.' Her lips twisted wryly. 'He's as judgmental as the next person.'

Well, she'd got over Jimmy, and she would get over Ross too. Soon there would be a new assignment. She would immerse herself in her work—being careful not to let herself become the slightest bit emotionally involved—and in time Ross would be no more than a memory.

She'd been back in the office about a week when Mr Anderson asked to see her.

'Ross wants you back,' he said without preamble.

The colour drained from her cheeks as she stared at him. 'I don't believe it.'

'He can't work with Sally.'

'You could send him one of the other writers.'

Hugh Anderson leaned back in his chair. 'He wants you, Kirby.'

Tension was a tight knot in her abdomen, and her throat was dry. 'I can't go.'

'You must.' His expression was kind enough, his words had the sound of an order.

Kirby looked at him, and then away. 'We just can't work together,' she said at last, a little desperately.

'From what I saw of your stuff you worked together very well indeed.'

It was true. But what was equally true was that they couldn't *live* together. In the same house. In the same space. Once it had been wonderful. Now it could only be a form of hell.

None of which she could explain to her boss.

'You don't understand,' she said uncertainly.

'You're right, I don't.' He brought his body forward. 'There are sparks that fly between you and Ross.'

Green eyes were wide. 'You know that?'

'From the beginning. From the day you first went to see him.'

'I didn't want to work with him even then,' she said, remembering.

'You were all agog when I handed you the assignment. And then you came back from that first meeting and asked me to send someone else.'

'Yes . . .'

'What you don't know,' said her boss, watching her face, 'is that before you walked into this office to talk to me Ross had 'phoned. He said that if you didn't work with him, nobody would.'

A tremor ran through her as she looked at him. Her chest was so tight that she could hardly breathe. 'Did . . . he give a reason?'

'No. Just as he hasn't given one this time.'

'That's why you were so adamant I go back.'

'Right. And I'm adamant again now.'

'No!' Kirby was on her feet, eyes sparkling with protest. 'I won't go!'

'I don't believe you have a choice.' It was said softly, regretfully almost.

'Why not?' she demanded.

'Dennis Demayne will hear of it if you don't finish the assignment.' He paused, then went on. 'You'll have lost your chance to work with him. Or with anyone else for that matter.'

It took a few moments for the words to sink in. Then Kirby said, 'I think you're holding a gun to my head.'

Mr Anderson spread his hands. 'I think I am.'

She looked at him, the light dying in her eyes. 'As you say, I've no choice. I'll have to make a few personal arrangements. I could go back to Ross . . . to Mr Dolby . . . on Wednesday.'

She was walking to the door when she heard Mr Anderson say, 'Kirby,' and she turned.

'I can only guess at the reason for the sparks,' he said softly. 'I do know they're producing what I want. It's going to be a lively book.'

There was compassion in his eyes now. Well, and why not? His blackmail had achieved his objective, he could afford to be gentle.

He said, 'Perhaps some day you'll tell me about it.'

So Meg went back to Lynn, and Kirby went back to Ross. As she drove the car along the winding coastal road she thought it seemed like a home-coming—and wished that it didn't. She also wished that she didn't feel so uneasy. True, she was only going back under duress, yet she dreaded the meeting with Ross.

What she didn't expect was that he would make it so easy for her. He must have been listening for her car, for by the time she was walking to the house he was coming to meet her.

Even before he reached her he'd put out his hands, and as he got to her he took her hands in his and said, 'I was worried you might not come. Forgive me, Kirby.'

She had missed him, she knew it the moment she saw him. He was so good-looking, so ruggedly appealing. And she longed so much just to let herself go into his arms.

But she was wiser now than she'd ever been before. And she'd learned her lesson. So she said, 'I nearly didn't come. Even though my boss held a gun to my head.'

'Thank God you did.'

She decided to ignore the remark, though it sounded heartfelt. 'Why couldn't you work with Sally?'

'Dreadful girl.'

'Nonsense. She's very nice. She's also very efficient, and she knows what she's doing. Unlike me, she's been ghost-writing for ages.'

'She refused to work without a note-book. She insisted on set hours.'

For the first time Kirby let herself smile. 'Well, good for her.'

And then Ross was smiling back at her, and she had to steel herself very hard to remain unaffected. She'd forgotten—almost—the little gold specks that shot the dark eyes when he smiled, and the laughter lines that ran in grooves along the sides of his cheeks to the corners of his mouth. She hadn't forgotten just how profoundly that smile was able to stir her.

'Who am I kidding?' Ross said. 'Sally wasn't you. That was what was wrong with her.'

She could feel the pull in his hands, but she took a step back. 'You were so angry.'

'Yes.' He looked suddenly tense.

'Ross Dolby, free-thinking spirit. So tolerant, so unconventional. Yet you had the nerve to judge me.'

'You've got it all wrong.'

'The hell I have. *Miss* Lessard. Do you think I've forgotten the way you said it? You were so contemptuous when you realised Meg was my child. A virgin had your understanding. A single mother only had your disdain.'

'You do have it wrong.' He was speaking very quietly now. 'I *was* furious, Kirby. Because I could only see that you'd lied to me. All the time you were pretending to be a virgin, you were so vulnerable, so frightened, I wanted so much to help you. Can you imagine how I felt when I saw you with your child? All I knew was that you'd made a fool of me.'

'That was never my intention,' she said uncertainly.

'I realised that when I cooled down. By that time you'd gone.'

She looked at him, wordlessly, not knowing what to say. Knowing only that she longed to be in his arms, and that the insanity of that longing seemed to make no difference to the feeling.

'That night on the beach at Fish Hoek ... Couldn't you tell I wasn't a virgin?'

'I remember wondering why you ... But we were both wet from the sea, and I was much too aroused to think about anything very much.'

She stared at him. Whatever arrogance there had been in the past, there was no sign of it now. Ross was always so sure of himself, so much in control. Yet at the moment he looked like a man who wanted very much to make amends. As for Kirby herself—all the way from Cape Town she'd planned the things she meant to say to him. Cold angry words. Yet now that she was actually with him she was filled with the most primitive female emotions, and the words were gone from her mind.

She drew a shuddering breath. 'I'll tell you about it.'

He put a finger on her lips, closing them. 'Not now, darling. There's only one thing we both want now.'

His lips and hands were sensuous, tantalising, undermining all the defences she thought she had built up against him. She knew she should resist him, but she couldn't. Not when she wanted him just as much as he wanted her.

His kisses were deep and hungry and demanding, driving her beyond rational thought to a level where the only need was fulfilment. Her responses were instinctive, born of a deep primitive need that drowned out the cold put-downs she had rehearsed. His hands were moving over her throat and breasts, setting every nerve in her body on fire. His hard desire only matched her own, she was making small animal noises of pleasure and pain without even realising it.

He insisted on carrying her to his bedroom. They made love with a frenzy that had been missing that night on the beach. Perhaps it was born of frustration, of missing each other, wanting each other so much that nothing else seemed important. Afterwards they lay together, exhausted but content for the first time in over a week.

At last Kirby said, 'His name was Jimmy.'

The long body stiffened slightly, but the hand that stroked her throat was gentle. 'You don't have to talk about it.'

'I want to.'

Ross raised himself on one elbow and looked down at her. 'I don't want you to have any regrets.'

'I won't.'

'You were angry because you thought I had judged you, and you were right about that. No matter how it hurts me to think of you in another man's arms—and it does hurt, my darling—a double standard is wrong.'

She smiled into the damp flushed face so close to hers, wondering how it was possible to be so happy. 'That's a long speech Ross. I'm supposed to be doing the talking.'

He looked back at her, his eyes dark and intent. 'Talk then.' His grin was wicked. 'Only don't make it too long. I've better things in mind.'

'Ross, you're greedy.'

He trailed a finger teasingly across one breast. 'Get used to it.'

She didn't want to talk. She wanted to make

love again. Ross isn't the only greedy one, she thought. But it was time to tell him about Jimmy. About Meg.

'It was three years ago. I was nineteen, he was twenty. We'd been going out for a while, and I . . . well, I thought I loved him. I didn't of course.'

She was silent a few moments, remembering. Trying to remember. Marvelling at the fact that Jimmy had become no more than a faceless name.

'What can I say, Ross? It shouldn't have happened, but it did. He said he loved me, that it was what people did when they loved each other. I was to blame as much as he was—I could have said no.'

'And then you found you were pregnant.'

'Yes. Can you imagine the shock? Just nineteen. No parents, no relatives to help me. Just a boy I didn't even know very well.'

'What was his reaction?'

'Sheer terror. Marriage was the very last thing on his mind. He had no money, he was in his second year at university. The fact that I had planned to study too never came up at all.'

'He didn't try to help you?'

After a moment Kirby said, 'I don't think he'd have been able to. And in the end it was for the best. An abortion was out as far as I was concerned. As for marriage—it wouldn't have worked. We found out too late that we meant nothing to each other. Meg would have been trapped between two parents who resented each other.'

'She's a pretty little girl,' Ross said.

'And a happy one. I've given her all the love that was in me.'

They were silent a while. Kirby lay quite still in

the hollow beneath Ross's shoulder, and he was stroking her hair.

At last he said, 'There's something I don't understand.'

She'd been waiting for that. 'My fear of sex. I didn't want to be hurt again, Ross. After Meg was born, after an initial period of real trauma, I finally began to get my life in order. I set up goals and priorities. University was out, but I could still have a career.'

'You were so cool and professional when you came here that first day.'

'You soon put a stop to that, didn't you?'

She wasn't angry. She couldn't be angry with him. She could feel him all around her, the tough hard muscles and sinews, the male smell of him. This was bliss, she thought.

But there were still things to explain.

'My career became important to me. It still is. As a means of giving us both a decent life. For my own self-esteem.'

'I can understand that.'

'What happened with Jimmy ... Well, it happened, and I'll never be sorry because I can't imagine life without my baby. But I made up my mind never to let anything like it happen again.'

She twisted her head so that she could see him. 'Not just the baby bit. The whole thing. Men. Sex. Feelings.'

Ross let out a soft whistle. 'I see. . .'

'No man was going to get close to me ever again. I didn't want to feel again.'

'But you do feel, Kirby.'

'Yes, I do.' She stroked the bare chest, loving the texture of the muscled body. 'You made sure of that, didn't you?'

'You're a warm, passionate woman.'

'I didn't want to be.'

'You can't change yourself.'

'You've taught me that. No, Ross ... not now ... I'm trying to talk.'

'You've talked enough,' he said lazily, but with a note of sensuous provocation.

'We're surely not going to make love again?' she said, over the growing hunger in her loins.

'Are you going to ration us?' He was teasing, but then his voice became husky. 'I would give anything to erase the past for you, Kirby. You were so tight and prim when I first met you. Remember the first portraits?'

'Dozens of Ross Dolbys on my pillow. Oh, yes!'

'You tried so hard to make me think that was how you really were, and all the time I knew there was a feeling loving woman behind that cool exterior.'

'Yes ...'

'But it doesn't have to be that way any longer. Everything has changed now.'

She was about to tell him that there were things that hadn't changed at all, but already he was kissing her, caressing her. He knew just where to touch her, how to arouse and excite her. And within moments she was lost to his lovemaking, and nothing else mattered. The only thing in the world was Ross, and the things he was doing to her, and the words he was whispering between kisses.

Later, much later, they got up and went for a walk on the beach. At the rocks where Ross had taught her to fish they stopped and sat down on the sand.

'When will you bring Meg to live here?' Ross asked.

'Is that what you want?'

'The sooner she gets to know her new father the better.'

Kirby jerked around to look at him, her eyes wide. 'Father?'

'Darling idiot. I mean to adopt her.'

'Ross . . . Ross, I don't think you . . .' The words seemed to be getting choked in her throat.

'Only after we're married, of course. When do you want it to be, darling?'

Shock was doing strange things to her system. It was hot on the beach, but Kirby's body felt suddenly frozen.

And then she managed to say, 'We've never even talked about marriage.'

Ross looked surprised. 'I took it for granted. After today . . . after all that's happened.' He must have seen her expression, because he smiled. 'Sorry, darling. I just thought you knew. But if you wanted a formal proposal, here it is. Darling Kirby Lessard, will you marry me?'

She didn't have to think about the answer. 'No, Ross, I can't'

It was his turn to be shocked. 'You must.'

'No.'

'I love you.'

Lord, this was more difficult than anything she had expected. Very gently, she said, 'I can't marry you, Ross.'

'Why not?'

'I thought I'd explained . . . There's my career.'

'I wouldn't stand in your way. As long as you didn't live with the chaps you were writing about, of course.'

'I have to be self-sufficient.' Her tone was suddenly urgent. 'It has to be that way.'

His eyes were hooded now, and there was a tightness in his jaw. 'Do you understand that I love you?'

'I didn't. I . . . I expect I was foolish. I do now.'

'I thought you loved me.'

'Love isn't for me, Ross. Please, please understand.'

'The hell I understand! What was it all about this morning if not love?' He was suddenly angry.

'Sex,' she said, trying not to sound tentative. This is an absolutely amazing conversation, she thought.

'When men say that kind of thing women get hurt. You were hurt yourself.'

'And you're hurt now, and I'm so sorry. So very sorry.' She sounded a little desperate.

'Is that all you can say?'

'You mean so much to me, Ross. More than any other man.'

'Not enough to marry me.'

'I value my independence too much. I can't just give it up.' She saw she wasn't getting through to him. 'There's so much I want to do for Meg.'

'I can give you and Meg everything you could ever want.'

'I know,' she said in a low voice. 'But, Ross, I have to do it on my own. That's just the way it is.'

'Then you don't love me,' he said flatly.

'We can still be friends . . .'

He made an impatient sound in his throat. 'Friends.'

'Lovers.' She put a hand on his arm and felt the rigidity of the muscles beneath her fingers.

He removed her hand. 'No.'

'Ross, please . . .'

'I don't want a mistress, Kirby.'

She flinched at the word. 'You've had lots of other women.'

'True. But you don't fall under the heading of "lots of women". I love you, Kirby, and I want you to be my wife.'

'Does it have to be all or nothing, Ross?'

'Yes.' It was said pleasantly enough.

'Then it's nothing,' she said, and turned away from him to hide her tears.

The next weeks were bitter-sweet. There was happiness in working with Ross again. He was more co-operative than he'd been at the start; willing to fill in the gaps in his biography, telling her incidents that were new to her.

And there was happiness, a kind of sheer joy, just in being with him. In the evenings, after supper, they walked on the beach or listened to music. Sometimes they fished, and if they were lucky with their catch then they *braaied* their supper on the sand. And sometimes they went for drives around the peninsula—to Cape Point where they watched the Atlantic meet the Indian Ocean in a thin line of foam; or to Kirstenbosch, where they walked through the lovely botanical gardens. Once they drove out to the wine-lands, and had a wonderful time tasting wines in the vineyards near Stellenbosch, then bought a few bottles to take back with them.

Much of what they did they had done before. But that didn't matter. They never seemed to get tired of each other's company, enjoying experiences together, laughing at a shared joke. All in all life was similar now to what it had been before Kirby had gone back to Cape Town.

Except in one respect. Ross never touched her.

Never tried to make love to her. That was the bitterness.

Kirby hadn't realised quite how much she would miss Ross's lovemaking. She was as much aware of him now as she had ever been. He had only to walk into the study when she was working for her heart to do a little somersault in her chest. When they walked together and his arm brushed against hers, she felt a small gnawing ache in her loins. It was becoming harder and harder to resist the urge to touch him. When they ate together, or when they sat beside each other in the car, the temptation just to reach out and put her hand on his arm was almost overpowering.

But something kept her back every time. Ross was as friendly as always, but so remote. It was as if he had detached himself from her physically. Which was what he had done, of course. Since the day she'd refused his proposal of marriage, a part of him had withdrawn from her.

There were nights when Kirby lay sleepless because she wanted him so much. One night she couldn't stand it any longer, and she went to his room.

He was awake too. 'Kirby?'

'Ross ... Ross, we can't go on like this.' She went to his bed, and all the time she was hoping that he would reach for her and take her in his arms, and make it easy for her.

'You've changed your mind?'

'Not about marriage.'

'Then go back to your room.'

'Ross ...'

It was too dark to see his face, but she heard the harshness in his tone. 'I'm a normal red-blooded man, Kirby. I can resist just so much temptation.'

'You don't have to resist,' she whispered.

'You know the answer to that.'

'Ross . . .' She heard the anguish in her voice, but she couldn't help it. 'It doesn't have to be this way.'

'It's the only way it can be.'

She felt humiliated and frustrated as she went back to her room. But more than anything else she was confused.

Was it possible that she was in love with Ross? Was that why she was so miserable? Why she had this need to be with him?

No! Vehemently she rejected the answer. True, she was fonder of him than of any man she'd ever met. She knew that there would never be anyone even remotely like him in the future.

But love? No, never that. Love was something you could control, she had to believe that. She had mapped out a future for herself, and love was not a part of it. And whether Ross liked it or not— whether Kirby herself was happy with the situation—that was how it must be.

And so when the book was finished she left him. She had expected the last days to be bad, but they were even more of an agony than she had imagined. Each hour became precious to her, and they were so fleeting. She wanted to hold on to every minute, every second, but the harder she tried, the faster they seemed to evade her.

All the while she kept hoping for some sign from Ross that he was relenting. She was leaving his house, but she didn't have to leave his life. She'd be in Cape Town, no more than an hour away from here. They could still be friends. Lovers. She could see no earthly reason why they must end a relationship that meant so much to them both.

But Ross was stubborn to the last. It had to be marriage or nothing at all. He didn't seem to understand her urgent need for freedom and independence, her will to make a success of life on her own. Kirby learned that she was stubborn too. It would tear her heart to say goodbye to Ross, but she would do it anyway.

Later she was never able to think back on the actual parting. As if by a tacit mutual consent they kept it brief. It was one of the most painful experiences of her life.

'Good luck with the new assignment, Kirby.'

'Thanks. It's been fun working with you, Ross.'

She was at the car when he handed her a package. It was flat and heavy and wrapped in thick paper.

'What's this?' she asked.

'Remember the painting?'

He'd said one day he would give it to her. 'I can't take it. Not now . . .'

'It's yours.' His voice was expressionless.

She was trembling. 'Ross . . .'

'Don't say any more,' he said harshly. 'Just take it and go.'

There were things she wanted to say, but her throat was choked with tears and her eyes were so blurred that she couldn't see his face. She got into her car, and drove off at a spanking speed that far exceeded the limit for the treacherous bends of the road. At the first view-point, where the road had been widened to allow people to stop and admire the spectacle of the Atlantic, Kirby screeched the car to a halt. Then she let the tears fall. She wept until it seemed there were no more tears left inside her.

At last, hoarse-throated and red-eyed, she

started the car once more and drove on to Cape Town and the next assignment.

Dennis Demayne was in interesting man. He had begun his career as a comedian pianist, and had been mildly successful in nightclubs and cabarets. Comedy was what he concentrated on, music was merely the medium he used to achieve it. Until the night a musician heard his act, and came backstage later with the advice that he should forget about comedy and concentrate on his piano-playing instead.

It was advice well taken. Gruelling years had followed that night, but today Dennis Demayne was a concert pianist with a devoted following. The musician who had heard his comedy act had not been forgotten, but had assumed an important role in Dennis's career.

Kirby felt that she should be able to turn out a readable book. Working with Dennis was very different from working with Ross. Dennis was eager for his story to be told. Unlike Ross, he had prepared a rough outline of milestones and anecdotes, he had a list of people he wanted mentioned, and he had a small folder of photographs which he wanted included.

Also in contrast to Ross, Dennis Demayne believed in a set routine, and he seemed to take it for granted that Kirby would take notes. He was organised and co-operative. Everything in fact that Kirby could have wished for.

If she was listless, Dennis was not to blame. It was not his fault that she had to summon every ounce of self-discipline to get herself writing. She tried very hard. There were mornings when her head ached and her eyes stung after hours of

sleeplessness, but somehow she forced herself out
of bed, and when she'd taken care of Meg and
dropped her off at Lynn's, she would make her
way to Dennis's apartment. There to work as best
she could. It had nothing to do with Dennis that
Ross haunted her dreams at night and invaded her
thoughts during the day. Dennis was entitled to a
ghost-writer who gave of her best.

Lynn, as good a friend as ever, was there when
Kirby understood that she had to talk or go crazy.

'I should never have agreed to work with Ross. I
should have insisted that Mr Anderson get
somebody else.'

You always knew it would be hard to leave
him.'

'I didn't think it would be as bad as this.'

Lynn was quiet a moment, and then she said,
'Do you regret the time you spent with him?'

'Yes!' Kirby looked at Lynn, and then her eyes
filled with tears and she covered them with her
hands. 'No . . .'

When she could speak again, she said, 'How can
I regret it? For a time there was beauty in my life
. . . richness . . . I mourn the fact that it's gone, but
I don't regret that I had it.'

'It's yours to have again if you want it,' Lynn
said softly.

'On Ross's terms.'

'Which any other woman would jump at.'

'Do you think there aren't times when I wonder
if I was fool to give it all up?' Kirby's expression
was sombre. 'I'm crazy about him, I know that.'

'Are you so sure you don't love him?'

'The only one I love,' Kirby said, 'is Meg. Lord,
Lynn, I'm so miserable, but I keep telling myself
I'll get over it.'

'How's the new book getting on?'

'Fine. Did I tell you that Dennis wants me to go to England with him? It'll mean leaving Meg with you again, but he wants me to see some of the places where he lived and worked. It's difficult to write about them without having been there.'

'You know you can leave Meg with me any time you like. I can't wait to have her again. Will you let Ross know you're going?'

'No.'

'Maybe,' Lynn said thoughtfully, 'a change of scene might be just the thing you need.'

'It's what I'm hoping.' Kirby tried to smile. 'I know I can't go on like this for much longer.'

If the change of scene did not make Kirby happier, it was certainly stimulating. She fell in love with London, was enraptured with the country-side, was fascinated with the places where Dennis Demayne had performed his comedy routines.

They were constantly on the go. By the time evening came Kirby was usually so tired that all she wanted to do was to stretch out in front of the television and relax.

She was half asleep on her bed one evening, when the newscaster's words jerked her to horrified wakefulness. '. . . when the accident took place. Ross Dolby is a well-known South African artist whose paintings are presently on exhibit in London. The seriousness of his condition is not yet known.'

A strangled gasp came from Kirby's throat, and then she was out of the room and banging on Dennis's door.

'Kirby?' He looked surprised to see her, dishevelled and half-dressed. And then he saw her expression. 'Kirby, what is it?'

'I have to go home.'

'There are still things to do . . .'

'I can't stay! Dennis, I'm so sorry. I'll arrange with Mr Anderson to send you someone else.'

'I'll wait till you can get back to the book. But Kirby, what's wrong? What's happened?'

'There's been an accident.'

'Your child?' he asked with swift concern.

'A man. Someone . . . who means a lot to me.' Kirby took a shuddering breath. 'Someone I love very much.'

Groote Schuur, home of the world's first heart-transplant, is a huge hospital, a sprawl of buildings on the slopes of Table Mountain. It took Kirby a little time to find Ross.

'Mr Dolby shouldn't be having visitors,' said the nurse.

'How is he?'

'Weak. He should be getting better, but there doesn't seem to be any fight in him. It's very strange.'

'Please, let me see him,' Kirby pleaded.

'Are you a relative?'

'A friend. My name is Kirby Lessard, and I . . .'

'Kirby!' The nurse's expression changed. 'He's been asking for you. When he was delirious he kept saying your name.'

'Then you'll let me in?'

A smile crossed weathered features. 'You might just be the best treatment we could give him.'

On the way from the airport Lynn had told Kirby as much as she knew about the accident. Ross had been driving home from Cape Town, it had been late and dark and a drunken driver had collided with him head-on. Ross's car had bounced against the slope of the mountain, he was lucky to be alive.

Kirby sucked in her breath when she saw him. He was very pale, as if someone had taken a cloth and washed the healthy tan from his cheeks. His eyes were closed, and on his face were lines that Kirby had not seen before. He looked drawn and haggard.

Was he asleep? She wasn't sure. Very quietly she walked to his bed, and touched his hand. If he was sleeping the gentle touch would not wake him.

For a moment he did not respond. And then his eyes fluttered open. Focused on her face.

'Kirby?' It was said uncertainly, as if he wasn't sure whether she was real or a dream.

'Yes.' She was trembling.

'You're in England.'

'I came back.'

'Why?' Ill as he was, there was authority in his tone.

She spread her fingers over the big hand. 'To be with you, my darling.'

He closed his eyes, and she waited. At last he opened them again. 'Say that again.'

'I came to be with you, my darling.'

'I can't believe it. I waited . . . always . . .'

He looked so weak that her heart went out to him. She'd never known how much she loved him. What a fool she had been.

'Hush.' She put a finger on his lips. 'Let me do the talking, or the nurse will say I've tired you and have me out of here in five seconds.'

He managed a grin. 'That won't do.'

'No, it won't. Ross, my darling, I came because I love you. I've loved you from the start, and I fought it because ... well, because I was stubborn.'

'You're crying,' he said.

She wiped a hand across her eyes. 'I know. Ross, is it too late?'

'It's never been too late. I always knew I was going to marry you. From the first day I set eyes on you. You were so serious, so prim. And so utterly lovable.'

'You're not supposed to be talking.'

'I'll say what I want. I told your boss it was going to be you or nobody. Nothing's changed.'

She couldn't believe what she was hearing. 'I love you, Ross.'

'I adore you, my darling Kirby. When are you going to marry me?'

She remembered what the nurse had said. 'When you start fighting and get the hell out of this place.'

The ghost of the old Ross was in the grin he gave her. Already, if that was possible, he was looking better.

'Kiss me, woman,' he ordered.

She kissed him, gently, tenderly, but with a hint of passion.

'Are you going to fight?' she asked.

'Better see about a wedding-dress, and a flower-girl dress for Meg,' he ordered. 'We'll be married in less than a month.'

And they were.

Harlequin Presents

Coming Next Month

887 LOVE ME NOT Lindsay Armstrong
A schoolteacher prepares to lead on an Australian boat designer. That's what she did to her sister, after all! But she doesn't count on his infinite charm—and her sister's deceit!

888 THE WINTER HEART Lillian Cheatham
After taking the blame for her sister's tragic carelessness, an artist escapes to Colorado to work as a secretary—never dreaming that her new boss chose her specifically.

889 A VERY PRIVATE LOVE Melinda Cross
While covering an Egyptian Arabian horse show in Kentucky, a reporter traveling incognito uncovers a reclusive American entrepreneur, also in disguise. He's the man she's been waiting for—to make or break her future.

890 THE OVER-MOUNTAIN MAN Emma Goldrick
A motorist stranded in the Great Smoky Mountains seeks refuge at the home of an inventor who imagines she's in cahoots with his aunt to end his bachelor days. What a notion....

891 THE MAN IN ROOM 12 Claudia Jameson
What with the blizzard and the flu epidemic at her mother's Welsh country inn, the man in room twelve is too much. And for the first time in her life, Dawn loses control of her emotions.

892 DARKNESS INTO LIGHT Carole Mortimer
The security-conscious new owner of the Sutherland estate warns his gardener against falling in love with him. But the only danger she can see is that he might break her heart....

893 FOREVER Lynn Turner
Can a surly ex-army colonel and a bogus nun find love and lasting happiness? Perhaps, with the help of a guardian angel to get them through the jungle alive!

894 A MOMENT IN TIME Yvonne Whittal
The shock of seeing each other again shatters the composure of a divorced couple. For her, at least, love lasted longer than a moment in time, though she isn't so sure of him.

Available in June wherever paperback books are sold, or through Harlequin Reader Service.

In the U.S.
901 Fuhrmann Blvd.
P.O. Box 1397
Buffalo, N.Y. 14240-1397

In Canada
P.O. Box 2800, Postal Station A
5170 Yonge Street
Willowdale, Ontario M2N 6J3